ACE II

ACE II

Arresting, Contemporary stories by Emerging writers

edited by
Julia Prendergast

RECENT WORK PRESS

ACE Anthology II: Arresting, Contemporary stories by Emerging writers
Recent Work Press
Canberra, Australia

Copyright © the authors, 2020

ISBN: 9780645008906 (paperback)

A catalogue record for this book is available from the National Library of Australia

Cover photograph: Jason Leung courtesy of unsplash
Cover design: Recent Work Press
Set by Recent Work Press

recentworkpress.com

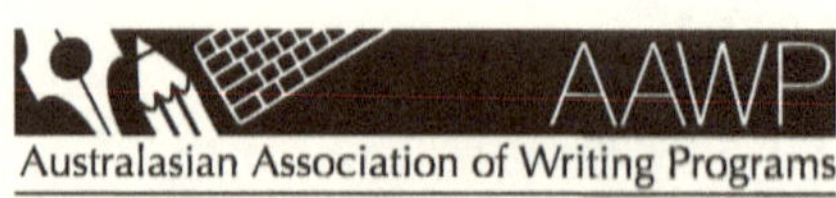

Contents

Introduction

Julia Prendergast

In each of the stories in this collection, the authors examine the conundrum and contradiction of human experience through carefully crafted narrative detail. The brevity of short-form fiction makes it an apt vessel for capturing the haunting incompleteness of human experience. Memorable short stories resonate because they are attentive to specificities and particularities: to detail as it relates to a distinct focalising consciousness. The authors in this collection employ narrative detail with intuitive hands and minds, fashioning an apprehended fictional world, an abstracted reality that resonates beyond the final lines of text.

As I worked with the authors featured in *ACE Anthology II. Arresting, Contemporary stories by Emerging writers*, I thought about what it means to 'handle' someone else's story material—a continuing conversation I have with myself. I considered how our writing is influenced by the work of other writers, as well as those who respond to our work. I'm deeply interested in the intersections— the frayed edges of our writing and reading minds. For me, the significance of working with other writers is implicitly tied to the act of acute listening—what conundrum of lived experience is the author contemplating?

Each story in this collection is marked by the urgency of idea, captured as raw sensory data. The stories are diverse and multi-layered. Collectively, they are attentive to the crucial relationship between idiosyncratic voice and sharply rendered detail, creating an experiential world that 'feels real' to the reader.

I am indebted to the authors in this collection, for the gift of editing their stories. As we engage with the work of other writers, we often encounter unresolved and perhaps irresolvable ideas. We bear witness to the writer's attempt to capture complex ideas in alterity, through the insightful handling of concrete and specific narrative detail. This is the great joy of reading and the lure of writing—encountering the otherwise unsayable through the deft handling of sensory detail, bearing witness to the creative use of language as an act of deep homage to an otherwise irresolvable idea.

I'm deeply interested in the way that writing and reading seems to function like lived experience, entering our own affect cycle, so that it's possible we might be altered by the stories that move us. I am inordinately grateful to have been altered by the stories in this collection. It has been my privilege and pleasure to listen acutely to these authors and to have had my empathic compass expanded by their art.

Byzantium

Joshua Kemp

His life is a shuffling deck of cards. Awareness boils up. Razor-tipped shards of terror, or astonishing wonder.

A tunnel of peppermint scrub. The path is endless. Feels like he's been trudging barefoot for hours, the light heavy in the dead tree limbs, a soft burn sears the yellow sky. The wind picks up, rolling across him. He grabs the flannel tighter around himself despite the heat, needs the long sleeves to hide the tell-tale bruising.

He thinks it's the sound of the Southern Ocean, a slow grumble behind him, but it's getting closer. Hoyle turns on the spot, wonder bleeding into fear. The channel of scrub quivers. A thimble of uncertainty in his throat, the grumble now a roar.

Lithe without shoes, he steps into the side of the scrub, quick as a scared rabbit. Only now realises how dark it's gotten, dusk bruising all through the wind-scarred trees, a beam of white, bouncing down the track. A single headlight, motorbike engine, wheels battling the loose dirt.

Hoyle feels the peppermints concealing him for the first time, and he flickers with leaf shadow. No one can see him. No one knows he's here, watching out of scrub-dark. For so long he's been seeing the world out of a victim's eyes. Now he can see it from the other side.

Waiting, hidden. This is what it feels like to be the predator.

The young rider has a helmet on, so Hoyle can't see his face. He rides the trail bike comically, both legs outstretched, away from the pegs. How easy it would be to step out at the right moment, whip him from the seat. The soft head inside the helmet fragile like an egg inside it's shell. If he was unable to control his thoughts before he'd started using PCP just a year ago, there was no hope since.

By the time he gets back to the cabin, hidden behind the wattles, the wind whips him harder, relentlessly. He doesn't go inside. He stands on the front deck, drinks in the Antarctic wind. There's no streetlights out here, no light at all. The coast blanketed dark. His life is a shuffling deck of cards, and right now he's more alive than he's felt in ages. To complete the moment, he presses the needle-bruises on his inner elbow. Likes the dull ache. It keeps the promise of his satchel at bay. Hoyle's no junkie. He's spare with it, meticulous.

He can still hear Kaitlin's voice so clearly, 'You're a functional user.'

He's been trying not to think about Kaitlin. Peers west, toward the national park, into all that ancient wildness following the coastline for hundreds of kilometres. Knows tomorrow he must step out into it, take a step back through the years, back toward Kaitlin and all the hollow she left in him.

He sees a buoy the other side of the wattles, riding the tumult of the Southern Ocean in the dark. It flashes, blue for a couple of seconds, and then dark again. Each time it winks on, he can see a cold shadow on the window glass. Waiting. Takes him a while to accept that shadow belongs to him.

He drives right past the road into the Lehmann homestead, eases his foot on the brakes in the gravel, slides. He backs up to the gate, stares down the long drive with the one-sided banksias nodding toward the ruined stone barn. Just a chain on the gate, so he lets himself through. The house is two-storeys. A ridge of red sandstone the other side of the heathlands. A forgotten pine plantation. West Mount Barren a blue shadow out there, further on.

She's leaning against the balustrade, under the overcast sky, as if expecting him. A black AC/DC shirt, tight jeans, no shoes. The same witch-black eyes behind a twirl of JPS Red smoke. Nothing like her older sister, in features, shape, demeanour. He watches her go back into the house.

She appears at the front door, lets him through. As she turns to go, he watches her fine, pale hands glide across the wooden frame. So small and fine it's like her fingers are built completely from wishbones. 'Thought you were gonna be here last night?' she asks.

'Got in late. Just went to the caravan park. Stayed in a cabin.'

'Didn't have to do that. Coulda saved ya a buck.'

The lounge room is a sty. She sits on the couch, readies another cig. He gets all parental, almost tells her she shouldn't be smoking that shit. But then presses on his inner elbow. 'Place looks nice.'

Sharni shrugs. 'I do what I can. Bit difficult with Dad out bush.'

'Where's he gone?'

'God knows. Some cave out in the middle of whoop-whoop. Said he'd only be a fortnight. That was a month ago.'

Hoyle watches her thumb at the lighter. She drags, her eyes get even darker. He didn't think that was possible.

'I'm not really sure what I'm doing here, Shar.'

'I told you over the phone.'

He gets up, goes to the window. Windy out there. The mallee-heath sways, crashes. The surface of it all shimmering like an angry sea. That knowing wildness watching him back through the glass. West Mount Barren, the only thing unmoved.

'I'm not a cop.'

'But you're a journo.'

'Not really.'

'What are you then?'

On the track last night, almost dragging that rider from his bike. Hoyle wonders.

'I write True Crime.' He takes a moment to consider this. 'Try to. I get fat off bored housewives and teenagers who want to read about the sick shit that's gone on in their neighbourhood. I'm like a tick.' He looks back at Sharni. 'I can't help her,' he says.

'That's bullshit.'

'She confessed. Told the cops she did it. You don't believe her?'

'Do you?'

'He was hitting her, wasn't he?'

Sharni hangs her head a little. 'A couple of times, yeah. That she told me about.'

'Well, you can only get kicked in the guts so many times before you kick back.' Hoyle turns to the mallee-heath again. 'Lotta men learn that lesson too late.'

'Not Kait. You knew her, better than anyone.'

'I used to know her.'

'Still do. You know, same as me. She couldn't do what she said she did. Not matter how bad he was laying into her.'

Hoyle rubs at his face irritably. 'Even if I did agree, which I'm not saying I do, I don't know what you think I can do about it.'

'I dunno, fuck!' she cries, spilling her packet of cigs all over the couch. 'Do whatever it is you do. To write your books.'

He turns to meet her eyes again, dark as a void. She stares him down.

'Just fucken…' She shakes her head, flicks the lighter again. 'Help her.'

The moon is fat like a gorged tick, making the house glow like a haunted mansion. The blue mallees rasping like racks of bones as Hoyle and Sharni make their way down to the barn in the dark. He walks behind her, can't help noting the shape of her small bum. Though she fills him with menace to see her with ear muffs around her neck, the shotgun in her hands. The roof of the barn is gone, so they squat in the lee of the eastern wall. The moon makes the globes of the prostrate banksias glow molten white like lanterns under the sea.

'You actually seen these wild dogs?' Hoyle asks. 'Or are they just a myth?'

'It's a fucken plague. Dad and I are out here most nights. Eight of them showed up at Dunn's place last week. He was fixing a fence. They tore him off the back of his ute. Not dingoes either. Big pitbulllookin’ cunts. Ripped him up bad. I went and saw him in hospital last week. Lost one of his pinkies.’

The cold wind tears into the open barn, but they share cans of Bundy to keep warm. Watch the dark heathlands. Hoyle notices a grave site at the edge of the Christmas trees. A dead settler. He watches for the eyes of their prey, red and blinking.

He wakes with her head snuggled into his chest. The delicate weight of her. He wants to kiss her forehead, her lips, her closed eyelids. Even the idea of it is a betrayal to Kaitlin.

The wind is cold as ever, shaking across the mallee-heath all the way from West Mount Barren. It juts out there like a dead volcano. He saunters through the prostrate banksias, their cones growing straight out of the sand, hugging the flannel to himself. He stumbles across the waterhole. The black cattle peer up at him, surrounded by the skeleton paperbarks, ghoulish hands reaching from the silvered mire. The earth salt-scarred. Hoof-bashed. The cows snort. Stinking fucken things.

He’s only sauntered a little further on when he comes to the depression, stares down at the huge shape lounging in there. The bull can’t be long dead, a matter of hours. Hoyle slips down the ragged bank of earth, kneels beside it, surveying the bite marks on its hide, its torn-out throat. The dark slather pooling around its mouth. He stands and hugs the flannel to him and tracks back to find the various prints left by dogs in the dirt.

He follows the hunters away from the waterhole, tripping and stumbling on the roots of the heath as he goes.

He's aiming to visit the beach where it happened. But finds himself heading out to the highway instead, turning at Jerramungup. Dry paddocks rasping golden in the sun. The odd black top of granite showing through scurfy earth.

When he reaches the eastern side of the national park, he takes the gravel track down through wiry heathlands. He parks at East Mount Barren, walks into the wind off the crashing sea. Rising amongst royal hakeas, stiff possum banksias. Snarly, hard leaves scratch his shins, open him up. He saunters up the ridge of white quartzite shining in the mountain, like a rib of marbly fat exposed in a cut thigh. The way his shoes sound in the pieces of it is like walking through scattered animal bones.

Escaping Sharni, the dead bull, thinking about Kaitlin. This is exactly what he needs. This is enough to convince him to unclench all the things he's holding onto. It's enough to make him consider driving out to the coast later on, taking out his satchel, lobbing it into the foamy breakers.

He comes to the looming outcrops of white rock, like the pale bellies of giant sharks, and tramps up through the hakeas with their red flowers like tiny, hairy roses. Snug between quartzite one side, and a wall of tall scrub the other, he lounges in brush-shadow. A ticking in the loose deadwood behind him, scuttling. He doesn't think much of it at first, just watches the wind on the mountain.

Now it's closer, he pivots on the spot, deathly white with sunscreen. Eyes watering from where the breeze rushes in. He peers into the bundled sticks. Knows this is dugite country. The scuttling continues, coming towards him.

Hoyle presses onto his feet, crouching. His tired knees creep under him, finding a rhythm he didn't know he was capable of. Before he knows it, he's eye to eye with a crevice skink. It freezes. They watch each other. The urban man having snuck up on the wild thing. Hoyle can't believe how easy it was. How quickly the tables can flip.

His PCP-fried mind does something weird then. He imagines grabbing the skink and chewing it's head off. Feeling the small bones crunch between his teeth, the wallop of warm blood filling his mouth. He blinks, sees the skink scurry away now. None the wiser. No idea it'd just been bettered by a drug-fucked idiot from the suburbs.

By late that afternoon he's built up enough courage to find the beach. He follows the highway back around to the western side of Fitzgerald River National Park, heads toward Point Ann. He follows the gravel road down beside the Little Boondadup River, until the beach opens at the end there. Sauntering down onto the anaemic shore, he carries his satchel in one hand.

There's an oyster catcher near the breakers. His chest swells to see it here. This tiny living thing alone in a swirling immensity of land and water. From here he can see the Central Wilderness, the Barrens, like the Holy City of Byzantium. That poem they had to read for uni, the old man travelling to the holy city to meet his death.

Hoyle watches the mountains in the distance. He could just wander out there, forget this, the burden in the satchel in his hand. Already he knows he doesn't have the strength, mentally. He's mind-fucked. Not even that resolute solitude, quartzite fog and mountain grey, could fix the millions of star-shaped wounds in his brain now.

As dusk turns a hard steely silver in the sky, shaping out the big dunes, Hoyle finds a place in the sand to consider his satchel. The oyster catcher follows the lip of the raging breakers, jumping back from the foam. It moves on, toward the Central Wilderness.

He prepares. Trying to harden himself for this. To break through the shellac of himself, jump into someone else. The tourniquet chews on his arm until his favourite green vein worms up. Needle-prick and thumb-plunge. All that time spent with Kaitlin years ago, maybe he always wanted to get under her skin. Now he finally has his chance to do just that.

He's gathered as much information as possible, from the police reports to talking to Sharni about the volatile relationship. And still, he has no idea what he's about to jump into. The PCP sets his imagination on fire, spelling out the sickly puppet show before his eyes.

They were staying for the night on the beach in their caravan. Apparently it was one of his favourite surfing spots. Him, the victim. Hoyle blinks and finds himself behind the stranger's eyes. Wayne Miller. Early twenties, younger than Kaitlin, once a champion on the local circuit, until he was introduced to ice. Was in and out of rehab a few times since. Since meeting Kaitlin, he'd got his head screwed-on. Mostly.

They were arguing. When they disagreed, she took this tone with him. She'd been to university, passed with flying colours. She liked to hang out with the drug-fucked animals from Margaret River like she belonged with them but she really reckoned she was better than them all.

She was shooting off at the mouth, and with four VBs in him, he was seeing red, feeling the sweat on his face. So he socked her one. Just the one. Not the first time. She dropped against the side-board, and he saw the blood running out of her mouth.

It was the tears in her eyes that got him. All that love came rushing in, all that love he sometimes forgot. He realised what he'd done, and he wanted to die for it.

Hoyle blinks again, in Kaitlin's skin now. A quick jaunt across the inside of the caravan, straight into someone else.

She couldn't believe it. He'd done it again. He made so many promises. It would never happen again, it was just the once. He'd say, 'I'm so so sorry, baby.' But then it happened a second time. A third. There were always plenty of excuses. The grog, her nagging. The way she talked down to him, just coz she was a few years older than him. She knew how this worked. She could see the pattern, like a fly shooting straight into a spider's web, and still she'd ended up here. Again and again.

That's when the hand reached for the gidgee. The silver gleam of its handle. Cold and salt-streaked. His eyes shone with surprise as the barbs plunged in his windpipe. A faint whistling of air. That look of surprise almost made her laugh as the hot fan of blood whipped across the inside wall. He gargled. All his love—stupid angry love— gushing from his open mouth.

When he finally settles in himself again, Hoyle sits up in the sand, like a peat-stinking mummy half buried by the wind moving the dunes over him. Billions of stars waver like pale firelight. The sea a huge stirring blackness.

He wipes the slobber from the corner of his mouth, tries to focus on the shape of himself again, finally letting Kaitlin go, her and then Wayne, after riding inside their bodies for the shortest time. Instead he thinks about that hand which reached for Wayne's gidgee, pale and delicate, as if built from wishbones.

Hoyle wanders outside the broken wall of the barn in the dark, peering back through the shattered stone. He can see Sharni propped up with the ear muffs hanging around her neck. The shotgun aimed at the ground, another night spent with an eye fixed on the dark for the wild dogs. Somehow he still doubts they'll show up, if they exist at all.

Watching her poised there, patient and cold, he sees it again, her hand on the gidgee. It wasn't something he could know for certain, after all what he saw was some PCP-induced fever dream. Kaitlin may have been in love with Wayne Miller, the man she confessed to sticking with his own gidgee. But there was only one true love of her life. And that was the little sister sitting in the ruined barn with the shotgun between her knees.

Hoyle freezes when his nostrils flex, a familiar smell. Dog-stink. His back to the mallee-heath and now he hears a paw-fall behind him. When he turns, Hoyle stares at the five shadows, wonders how he'll come out of this. After he's been tried by these different sets of teeth.

The wild dogs blink, eyes like blood-stars. And this is his test, to see how great and steely his resolve is.

All five are on him in a flash, all at once, and he starts to scream. He can hardly feel the mauling but acknowledges his forearm in a set of jaws. The head shakes from side to side, then rips back. Hoyle feels the skin of his hand strip off like a glove, his index finger comes away at the joint.

The first shotgun blast takes the furthest dog by surprise. It's loose head dangles on the ground from a tether of skin, before the body crumples after it. The other four let Hoyle loose, scampering for safety. Sharni perches above him on the stone wall, not bothering with the ear muffs. One of the dogs turns to meet her, intent on finishing Hoyle's trial.

She aims, wincing. The heathlands are silent again after the dull, booming echo. Red brains drip from a Christmas tree.

Hoyle props himself back against the wall, gasping and staring at the stub where his finger used to be. Sharni strips off her jacket, wraps his numb hand in it. Applies pressure, holds it tight in her trembling hands.

He forces a smile to reassure her. 'Guess they're not a myth after all,' he says.

Glory Days

Margaret Hickey

In his dreams he's flying fast, over low hills, far above trees and into the stars. He can see lights on the horizon and he's almost there, it's not a moment away and when he wakes, heart beating fast and a vision of glory, he doesn't mind because he's sure he's had a glimpse of what's to come.

Already he can see it: the crowded streets, the smell of perfume and the giant high-rises lit up at night like lighthouses. It's the prospect of work, of money, of friends and of the night. No more discussions about rain and cows, it will be all about novels and films and experience. Because that's what I can't get here he thinks: life experience. He's yearning for it. He's drowning here in a crusty dam and he must get out.

One more day till he finds out his ATAR score. It's mid-afternoon and he's in his bedroom, legs dangling over the end of a single bed. A blowfly buzzes overhead, making long, slow arcs about the room. He's spent a lot of time in this room since the end of year 12, sleeping mainly and sometimes thinking.

The fly dips in low near his face then heads across to the window where it rests a moment on the sill. The term ATAR sounds like something from another planet and he imagines himself in a brave new world, a hero of sorts, fighting for the common man. His ATAR will determine what planet he'll exist on and he's pretty sure that it will be a good one. Anything under 90 and he'll be gutted. ATAR, he says aloud. Then he makes his voice low and says it in a Darth Vader voice, *ATAR*.

His mother calls him and he farts loudly in response. She's at the door in a moment, telling him to go and get his father because it's time to go to Grandma's.

He grunts in assent.

'Ten minutes Rob,' she says. 'Get up now darl.'

His mother doesn't look too bad for 47, but the way she talks; it's like she's a character in some moron sitcom! He lets out a long, drawn-out sigh. It's a wonder how he came to be born in this family he thinks, and not for the first time. When, at school interviews, his politics teacher told his parents that his essay on the Russian revolution was the best he'd ever seen, they stared at him open mouthed. 'And to think', his father marvelled, 'he's never been further than Mildura.'

Later that night he'd tried to explain to them about his essay, how he'd argued that the intelligentsia inspired social democracy and bolshevism in Europe. But his parents just kept eating their sausages, laughing at how they must have been a pack of posers to call themselves *intelligentsia*.

Rob gives his shoes a sniff and puts them on. He'll be glad to leave this room. It's too small for him and there's a musty smell in it he'll be pleased to be rid of.

Outside the heat hits him smack in the face. It's a northerly blast with Wimmera dirt for shrapnel and he covers his face with his hands. The air clings to him and his thighs chafe with every step. A small whirly whirly rises up out of nowhere and angles its way toward him. He half thinks about racing into the midst of it as he used to when he was a kid, but it dies down quickly and the world is still again. There goes my excitement for the day, he thinks, and then he says *ATAR* again in his Vader voice.

All about him the land is dying. That's the thing about farms, he thinks, you're constantly reminded of death and never life. Calves drown in troughs, sheep get their limbs caught in barbed wire and they die, bloodied and covered in flies. Ewes bleat while foetuses hang out of them and foxes hover on the fence lines. Even his old man, face wrinkled like a sultana, looks half gone. He finds his father near the shed, up to his neck in some sort of animal shit, deliberating.

'Dad!' he shouts over the low din of the animals, 'Grandma's thing.'

His father raises his thumb in understanding, gives his lower back a rub and goes back to whatever it is he's doing. All the farmers around here are old, he thinks. It's like some sort of virus hits when people turn eighteen - young have to leave. He turns back toward the house.

The bird boxes that are supposed to attract the rare turquoise parrot are lined up hopefully beneath the sagging gums near the empty dam. No bird has even bothered to shit on them. They're tired sentinels from another era but his mother remains positive. *Once spring comes*, she says every year. She's always on about stuff like that. Always in the garden: planting, mulching, pruning, weeding. Native grasses and whatnot. His parents are mad for it. Nature! What good is it? Leave that stuff to David Attenborough and all the other old fogies, he's out of here. He goes back inside, returns to his room, lies down and waits.

They arrive at his Grandma's to find that there's already a paddock half-filled with cars from the district. When he opens the door to get out, slowly and with great effort, his father gives him a look. 'Wearing strides on a day like this!' he says. 'You'll be hot Rob.' This is a conversation they have had before. 'They're not strides,' he reminds his father. 'They're stovepipes.' Stovepipes are like jeans, but they're tight. Really tight.

'Stick that in your stovepipe and smoke it,' his mother says to his father and they both grin. That grin. Sometimes it's hard to catch what it means, but not today. He's seen them wink too, though that one is harder to detect. At the parent teacher interview for instance, after his father said, 'And to think, he's never been further than Mildura!' there may have been a wink. But maybe not.

His Uncle John comes out to the car to greet them. He's a big man and a confident one for someone who still lives with his mother. John slaps his father on the back, kisses his mother and then turns to him, 'Hot aren't you mate?'

He scowls. Tries to look cool.

'Rob's wearing stovepipes,' his father says solemnly.

'Too right they're stovepipes,' his uncle says. 'I could cook an egg on you.'

God how he hates this place. His parents walk inside and he wanders around the back. His older cousins, the vaunted draft nominees and some of their friends are already there, kicking the footy around. They're friendly enough in a kind of dismissive way, calling him over, asking what he's been up to, but he can tell they don't really care.

He hovers around the sidelines for a while before settling under a grey tree with a packet of chips. The shade offered to him is pitiful, but at least it's something. He looks around. The low hills that surround the yellow paddocks look charred and the late afternoon sky is a bleached blue, stretched thin, not a cloud in sight. It could drive a man mad to look at that scene every day. He thinks about what he learned in year eight history and the willingness of Australians from this area to sign up for war. Shit, he thinks, eyeing the parched trees and rusted woolshed –it's no surprise to him. If someone offered him a free trip to Egypt and Turkey, he'd be off in a flash no matter what the risk. He eats his chips. Shrapnel my arse.

A little girl runs up to him out of nowhere and bats a helium balloon toward him. She's a fat thing with ridiculous hair done up in coloured ribbons and bows and her name may or may not be Kayla. He catches the balloon and bats it back but a gust of wind picks it up and it blows away. It rises fast and high—way above the trees—and begins to travel across the paddocks.

'Sorry,' Rob shrugs, 'you can get another one.'

The girl looks into the sky at the small speck of yellow, escaping. Without warning she begins to howl, her mouth a red square of misery.

'You lost my balloon!' she sobs, her fat finger pointing at him. 'You lost my best balloon.' She's really crying. Her distress stupefies him. He doesn't know what to do. What are little kids *for*? 'Meanie!' the girl shouts, her breath coming in quick hiccups. 'It's gone and I'll never, ever get it back!' She's really cracked it and there's nothing he can do. Should he get help? He considers going to find his mother, when he sees a man walking over. As the man bends down toward the girl, saying something low and cajoling, he recognises him as a distant cousin. The girl sniffs loudly for a moment before running toward the house, her sobs becoming song-like as she darts across the grass and dirt.

The man straightens and looks at him. 'Scaring the kids are you?'

'I didn't mean...'

But the man is unconcerned. He leans his back against the gum tree and lights a smoke, the afternoon light casting a shadow across his face. 'They're all a bunch of spoilt brats in my opinion,' the man says, inhaling and exhaling like an elegant dragon. There's a slight accent in his voice. An unfamiliar drawl or lilt. Rob asks him where he is from.

'New York. London. Here I suppose.'

The man's shadow reaches out toward him and Rob feels an odd desire to rest his head on it, to lie on the dried gum leaves and feel the black coolness of the man's shape beneath his head. 'I'm getting out of here as soon as I can,' he tells the shadow. 'I've had it.'

The man gives a strange laugh. 'Well good luck,' he says. 'It's harder than you think. God knows I've tried often enough, but my best stuff, the stuff the critics all like, is when I write about here.'

'The critics?'

'Plays. I write plays for theatre. Some very good, mostly bad. Not really enough to make a living.'

Rob remembers now, there's a relation, a writer who got away. He searches for something to say. 'You must hate coming back—after everything you've seen. I mean, it must be so BORING,' he says, turning from the shadow to the man. That low laugh again. 'Oh I don't know. Sometimes maybe. But there's something about this place that keeps drawing me back.' The man reaches down and picks up a handful of soil, rubs it in his hand. 'This dirt', he says with a kind of wonder, 'it's all they want me to write about.'

The two of them stare out from beneath the tree. A dog runs past and a plane flies overhead, making slow progress in the big open sky. The man finishes his cigarette. 'Good luck with the city,' he says, stamping the butt on the ground with his pointy shoe. 'No doubt I'll see you back here for a funeral or something.'

'Don't count on it.'

The man says something he doesn't hear and throws Rob a small rock from the handful of dirt he's been holding. He's too slow to catch it and it lands somewhere in the dirt beside him and by the time he's located it and picked it up, the man has gone. He fits the rock carefully into the back pocket of his stovepipes.

As Rob eats the rest of the chips his mother walks over, her low heels making little dust puffs in the dirt. She tells him to go and see his grandmother before they go.

In a few weeks he won't have to do things like this. He'll be smoking in some dimly lit bar, watching a girl band or discussing Kant with friends. He has vague hopes of picking up. Rob follows his mother into the house and thinks about the man he's just met. It's hard to place him here in this spot. He's like a different species—the way he leaned against the tree, the way he moulded into it. The image stays in Rob's head.

Inside, there is no air. The blinds are drawn and the room is thick with the smell of old skin and something else, more vinegary. His grandmother is sitting on a chair in the middle of the room, a large television screen blaring in front of her. His mother turns the TV off and the old lady's head whips around toward them surprisingly fast, her throat coming a close second to the face, its long flap of skin the colour of raw chicken.

'Rob's going off to Uni this year!' his mother says brightly. 'He's waiting on his ATAR *score.' His grandmother's head falls down onto her chest. She may be sleeping.*

'And to think,' his mother says sadly. 'She used to make the best trifle this side of Hamilton.' His Uncle John walks into the room and nods at his sister's words.

'Won all the prizes,' he agrees.

His mother leans closer into the older woman's face and shouts, 'Rob remembers your trifle from when he was younger, don't you Rob?' His grandmother says something in a bubble of spit and they all bend in to listen. 'I think she asked if you still like trifle,' his mother says after a pause. 'You should tell her you do.'

'Why? She can't hear a thing.'

'Just do it,' his mother hisses.

What follows is a hideous few minutes of him yelling, 'I still like trifle!' into the old lady's face. Her yellowed skin is encased in deep, flaky wrinkles and she legit smells of piss.

'I still like trifle!'

His mother urges him to keep going till he begins to feel something like panic.

'I still like trifle!'

A river of sweat runs down the back of his stovepipes. Finally, the old lady jolts in her chair.

'No need to shout!' she says through rancid breath. 'I'm not in Sydney!'

'Not in Sydney,' Uncle John repeats chuckling. 'Not in Sydney!'

Overhead, the fan slowly spins.

Later that evening, his mother and father laugh about it.

'Not in Sydney!' His mother says. 'You can't make that stuff up.' She brings out a tray of cold beef sandwiches and a beer for his father who eats while watching the cricket, boots off and big feet resting on a stool.

For some reason, the tray enrages him. He's so cross he doesn't bother to say thank you when she brings out one for him. She's probably never even heard of Geraldine Greer or any of those other historical ladies, he thinks as he chomps gloomily on his beef and green relish sandwich. But it's probably not all her fault. The only books in the house are by Ken Follett and even though *Trinity* was a pretty good read it wasn't exactly life changing. Because that's what he's after, a life change. A break in the monotony, from beef sandwiches on trays and old ladies with skin like a half-cooked chook. He leaves the crust of his sandwich on his plate and contemplates it angrily.

'I saw that writer today', he says to his father. 'Your cousin.'

'Eh? Who?'

'Beryl's son,' his mother chimes in. 'Peter. Did you talk to him Rob?'

He nods.

'Peter? A playwright!' His father says. 'That's a good one. Remember that play we saw of his in the Chaff house, out the back of Denny's?'

'Oh yes!' His mother recalls. 'That was a nice evening.'

'Critics write about him,' Rob says. 'He must be good.'

'Critics!' His father nearly chokes with laughter. 'If you mean Denny's mother writing to the Gazette to mention that the play would have been better off as a musical to give it a *bit of life* then yes, he's had plenty of critics.'

'Beryl is so happy to have him back for a good while,' his mother says.

'He told me he lives in New York and London.'

'And so he does; that is, when he's not fruit picking in Shepparton or asking his mother for money. Playwright!' His father looks cross. 'Next he'll call himself an Orchadist Consultant.'

Rob finishes his crust, has a drink of water and takes his tray into the kitchen. He walks slowly to his room, passing a mirror in the corridor on the way. His face is a mottled red and his shirt clings to his body. It hurts him to notice that despite the sit-ups he does in his room most nights, there's still a padding of fat in each breast and the kids at school are right, his legs *do* look like wheat silos. His uncle was correct too, the stovepipes are uncomfortably hot and they don't suit him. They don't suit him at all. In his room, he sits for awhile on his bed. Then, with some difficulty he takes off his jeans, folds them and hangs them over a chair. The small rock given to him by the man falls out of one of the pockets and lands on the floor. He contemplates it for a second before kicking it under the bed. It hits the steel bedframe and ricochets right back, hitting him somewhere beneath his knee.

When he lies down, he hears the fly again, still buzzing around. It bangs against the window and hovers around the shades. He gives the wall a slap and it goes quiet. He stares into the dark until time seems to stretch and grow thin. Eventually he drifts off to sleep and his last thought before he does is not of the score he will receive the next day or the life he hopes to lead, but rather it is of the sobbing child Kayla—her face a plate of unchecked anguish and despair.

Note: An earlier verision of 'Glory Days' was published in Margaret Hickey's short story collection *Rural Dreams* (MidnightSun Publishing; 2020).

Hinterlands

Joshua Hayes

I returned to Australia after five years in Beijing. A friend let me sleep on his couch while I adjusted to the reverse culture shock and looked for a place of my own. I hadn't planned on seeing my family, if I could help it.

By my third day back I'd yet to acclimatise to the stillness and clearness of the air, the dryness of the heat and the whiteness of the people. Sometimes I'd yell out in Mandarin, just to hear something yelled out in Mandarin. My friend took me to a housewarming party, perhaps hoping it would speed my recovery. Certainly it felt good to be jostled again, even if the people were too tall and danced to music I didn't know.

Through the press of strangers I glimpsed a woman I recognised. She was sparer and rangier than I remembered, but it was her. The blonde highlights of five years ago were gone; what was left of her hair was matte black, shaggy and severely undercut. The one tattoo she'd had when I'd left for China was now part of a hodgepodge of feathers, hearts, trees and ammunition belts. She danced more with her shoulders than with her hips, with bent elbows and a broad grin. It was my little sister.

She lived in a satellite town that had merged with the city—an outer, outer suburb with factory lands on one side and scrub on the other. Her house was sparsely furnished. Her mattress sat on two sanded palettes that she'd found on a roadside. She had no couch and hers was the only bed in the house, so I slept as best I could on a beanbag in the living room. Most mornings I'd wake to find her cat Timor curled up on my stomach.

'Where's his collar?'

'He kept getting them snagged in branches.'

'You should be careful. Someone might shoot him, out here. And he needs a bell.'

'They don't work.'

We were downwind of a paper mill. On bad days you drank the smell with your morning coffee and ate it with dessert. But the rent was cheap, she told me, and teaching bushwalkers to bushwalk didn't pay as well as she'd like. I wasn't complaining. On bad days in Beijing the smog had reduced visibility to a metre and a half. They called it PM2.5. It caused birth defects.

We ate what she grew in her vegetable patch, or what she salvaged from supermarket dumpsters. For a fridge she used a Westinghouse chest freezer, its temperature regulated by a converter that she'd assembled herself. It was the only electrical appliance in the house and it only ran for an hour a day. For baking she had a wood brick oven that doubled as a kiln. For fun she had a wind up gramophone. Grudgingly, she let me plug in my laptop.

'I need it to job hunt.'

'Use my bike. There are a bunch of cafes in town that'd take you on for work experience, at least.'

'It doesn't work like that anymore. It's all done online now.'

'You won't know if you don't try.'

For a week I had my run of the house while she took bushwalkers into Wilpena Pound. I slept in her bed and divided my time between Gumtree, Facebook, Twitter, YouTube, 9GAG and PornHub. On the morning of the second day Timor left a dead Rosella on the doorstep. I considered tying bells to his legs, but the thought of him pinioned in a tree deterred me.

If I went out it was to water the veggie patch or visit the supermarket. I gravitated to the dairy section, for five years in China the thing I'd missed most had been Pura chocolate milk, but I stocked up on wagyu beef and lamb sausages, too. My sister had barred me from bringing meat into the house and I was determined to have my fill of flesh before the week was out.

Timor became my confidant. I practised saying the things I one day hoped to say to my mum. I bought him fancy cat food and massaged the scruff of his neck when I felt guilty. On the fifth day he brought me another dead bird and I resolved to keep him indoors. I bought kitty litter, cut a cardboard box in half and spent an hour scrubbing his shit out of the carpet.

My sister returned in a thirteen seat Toyota Commuter. She parked it in the vacant lot next to the house and honked its horn.

'All aboard!'

The interior was cold, clean and grey. I stood bent beneath its low ceiling.

'Is this the University's?'

'Some friends' and mine.'

'It's in real good nick.'

'Yeah.'

'What's it for?'

'Project.'

She stared into middle distance, squeezing her bottom lip between her thumb and forefinger.

'How's the house hunt going?'

'Okay.'

'So... You've been here ten days. I figure, two weeks is a reasonable amount of time to put you up. If you could be out of here by Sunday... You'll probably have somewhere by then, right?'

'Uh-huh.'

'Things are gonna get kinda crazy here, next week. I'll have people over. A lot of people.'

'A party?'

'No. It's...' She shrugged and shook her head. 'A group.'

That night I ate sausages to spite her. I spat the gristle onto my plate while I searched Gumtree for flat sharers, typing messages with violent keystrokes. She seemed unaffected. She offered me tea.

'I've got Earl Grey, Buddha's Tears, lapsang souchong, ginger, or rooibos.'

'What other of Buddha's bodily fluids do you have?' I asked over my shoulder.

'You name it, we got it.'

Timor slinked past me and met her in the kitchen, arching his back into her calves. She muttered something.

'What?'

'Nothing. I see you gave him a kitty litter box.'

'Yeah. Better he stay in here than be out in the hinterlands.'

'Sure.'

On Friday night her girlfriend came over. Her name was Hannah. Her face was pale and lean and hard. She'd brought a box of vinyls and I sat flipping through them, not recognising any of the artists.

'What's Big Black like?'

'Halfway between punk and industrial. I'll play some.'

An awful sound filled the house, like someone beating a guitar with a lead pipe.

'Jesus...'

'Yeah. Not for everyone,' She removed the needle.

'I used to play Stravinsky in the car,' I said. 'To and from school. Really loud.'

My sister groaned.

'Whenever we got within five hundred feet of school, she'd curl over in her seat, ashamed to be seen with me.'

'I'm still ashamed.'

'You lived in China?'

'Yep. Five years.'

'Wow. What were you doing?'

'Teaching English.'

Her tongue stud clacked against her teeth as she mulled me over. 'It's pretty bad over there, hey?'

'In what way?'

'In most ways. Like the air. You have to wear a mask all the time, right?'

'Not every day, no. There are worse places. Mumbai's much worse. China's becoming more and more stringent with its air standards.'

'Not stringent enough.'

'Well—'

'How's the standard of living?'

'It's good. The company sets you up, helps you acclimatise and finds you a—'

'Sounds like they baby you.'

'Have you ever lived abroad?'

'Yeah.'

'Where?'

'Bangladesh.'

'How long for?'

'Six months.'

'Like a long holiday?'

'No, not really. I was working in a women's centre. Saw some pretty brutal shit.'

'Huh,' I played with a record sleeve.

'Bangladesh is an amazing place. Awful, but amazing.'

'So's China.'

In the morning I woke to find Hannah and my sister digging up the veggie patch. Hannah churned up the earth with a mattock, the muscles in her arms and shoulders bulging. My sister tossed the broken plants onto the compost heap.

'What are you doing?'

'Chucking this shit out,' Hannah wiped her brow with her forearm.

'We're planting native species instead,' my sister told me.

'Why?'

'Ever been to South East Asia?' Hannah dropped her mattock.

'Yeah, Thailand.'

'From Thailand to Bali, even into the heart of Borneo, know what you see?'

I shook my head.

'Palm oil plantations. That's it. No ecosystems, just a product,' she gestured to the compost heap. 'Consumables.'

'Yeah, we're not in Borneo.'

'Ever been to Queensland?'

'We're not in Queensland either, Goddamn it. Why'd you get me to water these plants if you were just gonna tear them up?'

My sister took off her gardening gloves and squinted at me.

'I mean, the water's precious, right?' I said. 'God forbid I waste the precious fucking water.'

'Dude...' Hannah scoffed and picked up her mattock. I went back into the house and opened my laptop and tried to ignore the sounds of roots snapping.

I went to the supermarket in the afternoon. When I returned to the house it was empty, though the Toyota was still in the vacant lot. I set out along a sagging chain link fence on the edge of the derelict gasworks, scanning the distant tree line for signs of movement. The trees seemed stunted, their trunks were black. I wondered if they were eucalyptus or some kind of wattle. I crawled into the gasworks through a hole in the fence and spent an hour exploring the narrow spaces between the benzole tanks and the purifiers.

I was on Facebook when my sister came back. It was almost seven.

'Any luck?' she asked.

'Have you seen Timor?'

'No.'

'You left a window open.'

'Did I?'

She went into the bathroom and started the shower. I could hear her voice through the hiss of pressurised water. After five minutes she shut off the water and emerged from the bathroom in her pyjamas, shaggy hair dripping.

'What were you singing?'

'Nothing. Big Black.'

I closed my laptop. 'You shouldn't let Hannah tell you what to do.'

She sat at the edge of the dining table and stared down at me.

'She doesn't.'

'Why'd you tear up your veggie patch?'

'I'm planting native species, instead. Acacia, karkalla, muntries. All edible. I won't have to water them.'

'You still water yourself.'

'Jesus Christ...'

I laughed, 'Lighten up.'

'What are you gonna do tomorrow?'

'I'm still looking.'

She stared into middle distance.

'You can stay here,' she said finally. 'A bit longer.'

'Thanks, sis.'

'You probably won't like my friends very much.'

'I'll try.'

'Please do.'

They sat on the floor drinking someone's home brewed beer. There'd been four, Harmony and Riven and someone and someone, all of them dreadlocked, hemp-clad and smelling of sweat and ganja, and I'd retreated to the patio with my laptop after introducing myself.

'Your sister's fucking awesome,' one of them had said.

'Yeah, she's alright.'

From outside I could hear them laughing. Hannah put a record on the gramophone. I plugged in my headphones and listened to Simon And Garfunkel, each mournful pop ballad weaving tenuously through the industrial clangour. I imagined the others liking my music more than Hannah's.

After the music had finished a new arrival came outside and introduced himself. His name was Ben. He was clean-shaven and wore glasses.

'So, what do you do?'

'I'm a hunter.'

'No way. Big game?'

He smiled and shook his head, 'Not trophy hunting.'

'Ah.'

'Heard you lived in China.'

'Yep. Five years.'

'Ni hao.'

'Ni hao.'

'That's all I got.'

'Me too,' I laughed. 'Not much more, anyway.'

'What's it like being back?'

'Shit,' I surprised myself.

'Well, that sucks. Why'd you leave?'

'I don't... It felt like I was treading water. Kinda why I left Australia in the first place.'

'Must be good to see your family again, though. Old friends.'

'Sure. Fucking hell, though, shit's expensive.'

A young woman wandered onto the patio. She was small and tan and pretty. Her hair was in a ponytail.

'Hey Ben.'

'Hey Amelia.'

Ben introduced us.

'Right, the brother,' she smiled. 'What do you do?'

'I'm a teacher,' I decided. 'You?'

'A vet.'

'Cool.'

'Is Ron coming?' She asked Ben.

'Yeah, I think so.'

'You'll like Ron,' she said to me.

'Everyone likes Ron,' Ben said.

'Well, not everyone...' Amelia laughed.

'What's his story?'

'He's a conservationist,' Amelia told me. 'Had a sanctuary in the Hills. One of a kind, really. It's all closed up now.'

'You worked there?'

'Yeah, with Luke and Harmony.'

Hannah and Riven walked out holding paint cans.

'We're painting the van,' Hannah said.

'I'm alright.' Ben smiled. I looked absently at the kiln.

'Come on,' Riven said to Amelia. 'It'll be a bonding experience.'

'Yeah, okay.'

They crossed the patio to the vacant lot, my sister following with the others.

'Ron oughta be here soon,' Ben said. 'Then you can see some guns.'

They painted the Toyota in camouflage colours, brown-greens and green-browns. Ben and I drank beer and watched from the patio.

'It must be pretty exhilarating, tracking something down, getting it in your sights.'

'It can be. I'm in a chopper a lot of the time.'

'That'd be amazing.'

'Gets your blood pumping.'

'What do you shoot?'

'Roos and brumbies. Camels, sometimes.'

'I was gonna get a gun license. More for the license than the gun. I grew up on a farm.'

'Yeah?'

'Yeah. Then I moved to the suburbs. Wasn't much point.'

It was late in the day when my sister's last guest arrived, a stout, elderly man with a bushy white beard and a misshapen fur hat.

'Looks like Davy Crockett and Father Christmas had a love child,' I said to Ben.

'That's Ron.'

'Ho-ho-ho!' He called out. I wondered if he had heard me. He carried a duffel bag to the dining table before turning to my sister.

'Hello, sweetheart.'

'Hi Ron.'

They embraced.

'Now, the presents,' he unzipped the duffle bag and took out a hunting rifle. 'For our crack shot,' he handed the gun to Ben.

'This is a Shilen,' Ben told us. 'Unloaded, don't worry. Good for beginners.'

'Here's the Remington,' Ron held up a second rifle. 'Thirty-ought-six. Better for bigger game. And some of these bastards get big, believe me.'

'What are these for?' I asked Amelia.

'The cats. Didn't your sister tell you?'

'No,' I watched Ron take out a third rifle, then a fourth, then a fifth. I studied his ugly fur hat. It had tabby markings. Its eyes were empty slits.

'That's a cat.'

'Yeah,' Amelia chuckled.

'That's disgusting.'

'It's not, really. If it was killed humanely and its body's been put to some use. What's disgusting is the number of native birds and mammals that thing probably killed before Ron shot it.'

I turned and walked to my sister.

'Where's Timor?'

'Dunno,' She wouldn't look at me.

'Where the fuck is Timor?'

The room fell silent.

'Not now,' my sister said.

I walked outside and stood on the bare earth where the veggie patch had been. Inside, Ron said something and someone laughed. I went to the compost heap and dug through the corn stalks and watermelon vines.

'I buried him.'

She was standing behind me.

'How'd you do it?'

'An injection. He didn't feel—

'That's fucking psycho.'

'What did you do with the birds he killed?'

'What?'

'You dumped them in the rubbish. With your cup noodles and your coke cans.'

'He was your cat.'

'Yes, he was.'

'I kept him inside, I fed him. He wouldn't have killed those birds if you bought him a fucking bell.'

'I could've given him three bells and he'd still kill a bird every week. It's really none of your business, though. He was my cat, I put him down.'

'You're such a fucking hypocrite.'

'No, I did this because I'm not a hypocrite.'

'You okay?' Hannah stood in the doorway.

'You don't know a thing about what's going on in this country,' my sister told me. 'There are millions of them out there. You understand? You can't name a single species of animal native to this region that isn't on the fucking endangered list.'

'Yeah, that's people.'

'And people have got to do something about it.'

My sister's guests had gathered at the screen door.

'One of these cunts gave you the needle, didn't they? It was that fucking vet.'

'Just leave.'

I walked to the house.

'No, *leave*. Get your shit tomorrow. We'll be gone in the morning.'

I slept in a motel and returned in the afternoon. The house was locked and empty. I took a shovel from the garden shed and dug up the veggie patch. She hadn't bothered to put him in a box. His eyes and mouth were caked with dirt. I used the spare key and brought him into her room and laid him out on her bed and covered him in her sheets. In the kitchen cupboard I found a five-hundred gram bag of salt. I carried it outside and shook it out over the veggie patch.

I turned the soil until the white grains had disappeared and I took the bag with me when I left.

I flew into Guangzhou a week later. The crowds and the smells and the smog felt alien to me. I found myself harried by the language and oppressed by the constant staring, but I had a job and that made everything easier.

Walking to and from the school I'd pass a narrow alleyway filled with street food vendors. After the first day I began fixing my eyes on the road ahead, but sometimes I'd glimpse the skinned bodies swaying on their hooks as a vendor shifted his cart. Occasionally I'd see them being hauled to and fro in cramped, chicken wire cages, mewling, hissing and spitting.

Sometimes I'd think about my sister burying acacia seeds in the barren soil and waiting for them to grow.

Kelpie

Deb Wain

She felt as if she had only just fallen asleep when the incessant barking of one of the dogs woke her. She could tell by the tone of the bark that it belonged to the pup. And she knew from previous nights that it didn't know when to quit. She lay still for a moment, willing the disturbance away, knowing it was futile.

She waited a little longer hoping that Jack would wake and go instead. The barking continued but he didn't rouse. A gentle nudge in his back with her elbow caused a falter in his snuffling snores but he soon settled back to the heavy exhalations of sleep. She realised this is what it would have been like if they had been able to have children; he would have slept through everything and she would have been up at the slightest noise. She sighed and flipped her side of the covers into the middle of the bed.

She didn't bother with her dressing gown; her body was warm from the heavy quilt and the proximity of Jack's heavy body. The barking stopped as she reached the bedroom door. She waited in the quiet darkness, reluctant to go out and disturb the pup if he had settled on his own but just as reluctant to turn back. The pup was a good working dog and a quick learner. They were able to get in before the auctions and pick him up for a song by calling in a couple of favours from Beryl, the breeder and trainer. She owed them. Jack had mended a couple of Beryl's fences, replaced a few rotted stumps under the house, things Beryl would've had a go at herself in her heyday but not anymore. She said the pup was the best from that litter.

They needed a reliable dog, one that would make up for the two stationhands they'd let go. Cattle prices had dropped and there was no news of rain coming any time soon. Jack and would crack open beers and talk over the news broadcast focusing on busy cities, or worse, Canberra. He only listened silently during the weather forecast. When news of international events took over the small square screen Jack would reach for the remote and turn it off. She watched as the image blinked away, wiped the crumbs from their afternoon toast and brisket into her open palm, and threw them out the back door for the little birds.

Outback Queensland sounded beautiful and romantic when he'd talked about it. They had been sitting in an Adelaide bar—he was between the wedding ceremony and the reception of a mate's wedding; she had just finished her shift at the hospital and had stopped off for a drink with friends. She hadn't realised how hard it was all going to be or how alone she would feel, entranced as she was by the contrast between his white teeth and his tanned face.

When they started dating, there was so little time. He came to town with his father to meet up with the family's stock agent and when his father returned to their station, he stayed for a week. Then two. Eventually, he had to go back. They wrote to each other—a chaste and papery courtship. They asked each other questions and waited weeks for the replies. What's your favourite food? Would you ever consider living here? How many dogs do you have? Do you want to have a big family? She took a job at the closest hospital to his family's station, at the Tibooburra Health Service. Later she would go back there, after they were married, towels bloody beneath her as she lay cramping in the back seat. He drove, looking back too often to be safe and telling her she was going to be all right, telling her they were nearly there.

After the first time, they both worried less. The preganacies came and went. Each time the scraping ache was the same. The hollowed out feeling was the same too and the tears caught her by surprise when she was sure she wasn't even thinking about it. She refused to show it, learning how to be wooden. When she was allowed to go home, she hugged her jacket or her bag across her chest as they pushed through the hospital door into daylight that was too bright, walking to the car under a sky that was too blue. He always opened the door of the ute for her to climb in.

The floorboards were cold against her warm feet. The barking didn't start up again but still she lingered in the bedroom doorway, remembering. When they collected the pup from Beryl's place in town, the old girl had picked him up by the scruff of his neck and dropped him into her waiting arms. She had carried the pup, cradled against her chest. She was about to get into the cab with him. Beryl snorted but said nothing. Jack said, 'Put him in the back. He'll have to get used to it some time.'

'Already used to it,' Beryl confirmed.

The pup had watched the old woman intently from the tray of the ute as they drove away.

Beryl turned and, without waving, went back inside the house, letting the screen door slap closed behind her wiry old back. Twisting around in the passenger seat, she watched the pup watching Beryl, his ears strained skyward. She felt an unexplained pang when the dog finally lay down on the tray and rested his head on his paws. She wanted to watch him all the way home but she turned to face the corrugated gravel road, pressing her back hard into the seat.

Now, standing without slippers on the bedroom floorboards, her feet were cold. The skin on her bare arms was cooling in the night air but there was no more barking. She padded back to bed.

She pulled the covers over her shoulder. Jack says that she spoils the dogs. They are meant to earn their keep. As far as she's concerned, they do. Bess, an older kelpie, would run all day if he needed her to, only collapsing against the back of the house or in a favourite patch of dirt in the yard when Jack goes indoors. She looks completely relaxed until he returns and her eyes follow him, ears pitched, almost touching above her head, waiting for the gesture and whistle.

She shifted her body under the covers and rested her back against his warmth. What she had really wanted was a house dog, a pet that she would be allowed to spoil. Something small, and preferably fluffy, that she could hold on her lap as they sat in front of the television of an evening, a comfort while watching the late news for an item about live export because nothing else—political upheavals, international catastrophes, horrific traffic accidents—means anything, out here. He couldn't see the point of a lapdog. She imagined burying her fingers in a brushed and washed coat, feeling the heat of the skin beneath. The working dogs billowed dust when he patted their sides, more of a thump than a stroke. His hands were always dirty anyway so he barely even noticed but she would go straight inside and wash hers after patting them. She couldn't stand the grime that was left on her palms and the tips of her fingers.

As she let her head sink back into the pillow, the pup started up again. 'Shit,' she hissed.

'I'll go,' he said, suddenly alert as if he had been awake all along. She heard his footfalls on the floorboards. The loose board further down the passage creaked under his bare soles. The backdoor clicked open and he spoke quietly to the pup. She couldn't make out what he was saying; it didn't sound like human words. It was a lilting thrum, like rain on a gust.

Kanreki

Anne Hotta

Megumi Yoshida had avoided her husband for several days. Perhaps it was the approach of her sixtieth birthday. Perhaps it was something else, something she'd let brew. On the fourth evening, however, she entered the formal tatami room. She knelt before the miniature altar and tapped on the brass singing bowl to get her husband's attention. 'Well,' she began. 'The weather's awful. Hot, sticky. The rains can't be far off.' She paused. 'It's National Eel Day. After dinner, I'll bring you some.'

His lips were unsmiling. In the months before his death, however, Minoru had often smiled. Timorous, secret smiles. Behind his newspaper, into his bowl of soup, out the window. Whenever he thought she wasn't looking.

She took up the duster, flicking it over a bottle of his favourite sake, a packet of dried squid, then the urn and another cursory swirl of feathers. After the cremation, she'd taken the funereal chopsticks, selecting a few small bones from the ashes to take with her, thinking they may be from his hands. What was she thinking—her husband wasn't one for touching or stroking.

'As you know, it's my kanreki soon.' She put the duster down. 'My new life.' She clasped her hands together to steady them, and looked him in the eye. 'You started a new life, didn't you, Husband? One you didn't tell me about.'

A few days later, in the private dining room of a traditional restaurant, Megumi's son, Jun, handed her a small box. 'Here you are, Mother. For your kanreki.'

Lifting the lid, she saw a red beret buried in white tissue.

Red, the colour of the screaming newborn. As a sixty-year-old, she'd lived through all twelve zodiacs in each of their five elemental phases, a complete life cycle. Now she could start another.

'Why don't you try it on?'

'Yes. After we eat.'

'Don't you like it?'

'Of course, I do.' She lifted up the tissue. 'It's kanreki. I don't know if I want it.'

Kumi, Junichi's wife, giggled. 'I don't think you have a choice, Mother. Why don't you wear the beret to your dance classes?'

Kumi had gone too far; Jun shot her a look. Megumi seized her chance.

'I never thought of that, Kumi san. What a clever girl you are.' She turned to her son. 'Does that mean you're okay with me dancing, Jun?'

'I didn't say that, Mother. You know that Father...'

'Wouldn't like it? No, I'm sure he wouldn't. But Father's no longer with us.'

She sipped some warmed sake. Trust Jun to take Minoru's part. Doesn't he wonder why his father collapsed and died in an out-of-the-way subway station late at night?

'We know you have to have some hobbies, Mother, but an older woman in Japan dancing? What about ikebana or a book club?'

'I like dancing, Jun. Don't worry, my heart is strong.'

She looked at him, slightly unnerved, realising as she spoke that Jun was about the same age as her dance teacher.

'To your new life then, Mother,' he said.

Megumi smiled. Kato sensei, unbelievably handsome, his chin resting on her hair, as he led her, his hand splayed on the small of her back.

'Yes,' she said, raising her cup. 'To my kanreki.'

She dropped her shopping bags. Then she shoved aside the bicycle standing on the porch so she could get to the front door. Junichi and Kumi lived on the first floor and Megumi on the ground. They shared the main entrance.

'I'm home, Haru. Where are you?' A small, scruffy terrier emerged, twirling about her like an over-dosed hamster. She cajoled the little creature into sitting on her lap where she stroked its tummy and checked her email. Mrs Kashiwa from her dance class, wanted to have coffee. No doubt she wanted to discuss a strategy for landing Kato sensei, Kashiwa san being the only student bold enough to openly proclaim her admiration. Megumi was sorry, but she was too busy for coffee.

Then there was her sister-in-law, Saori. *I wonder what you have planned for my brother's anniversary. Shall we meet somewhere and go to his grave together?*

A few days later, she met Saori and they went to the cemetery.

'You look so young, Megumi,' Saori remarked as they walked back to the train station. 'Are you having an affair?'

'Heavens, no,' Megumi laughed trawling through her handbag hoping to find her fold-away fan. The air hung wet and heavy. The two women stood a while in silence, only the indolent swishing of their fans, the caw of a single crow.

Then Saori spoke: 'I've never thanked you, Megumi, for being such a good wife to my brother. I know it wasn't always easy.'

Megumi was caught off guard. Was it merely an older sister's formal appreciation, or did she know something about her brother's kanreki?

'It was nothing,' Megumi mumbled. 'Don't mention it.'

Saori sighed. 'When all's said and done, what can women expect from men? Even in these modern times?'

'I suppose it depends on the man,' Megumi replied. 'Maybe we should choose more carefully.'

Her cheeks burned. Saori would know her marriage to Minoru had been arranged.

There was barely any breeze. In the dance studio, mascara bled and energy flagged. Then Kato sensei introduced the Tango. At once, fans were cast aside, skirts ruffled and like six parakeets, the women lined up, thrilled to be learning the Dance of Love. Like Megumi, these women had never danced in an intimate way with a man, even their own husbands. They only danced with each other, with Sensei and in their heads. The Tango was all they thought it would be.

'Yoshida san, please.' Sensei held out his hand. 'We will dance.'

With poise, she stepped towards him. They began to glide, moving as one, Megumi resting easily in his arms. He didn't ask for a pause in the music and they repeated all the steps. He added a turn, thrusting her from him. She feinted and dismissed him, only to allow herself to be caught and taken back into his arms. He pulled her in close. Her hands, breasts and thighs, all pressed up against the body of a man who wasn't her husband.

The music stopped and the dance was over. Megumi was unable to move.

'Magnificent, Mrs Yoshida,' he said. 'Magnificent.'

He stepped away and she pulled herself together. The ladies smiled sweetly; they knew it was well done even if their hearts were broken.

'You've certainly found your feet, haven't you?' one remarked later in the change room.

'Found Sensei, wouldn't you say?' Mrs Kashiwa retorted, executing a grandiose flourish in Megumi's direction.

'Don't say such silly things,' Megumi replied with an awkward laugh. She continued to shove her clothes carelessly into her bag, desperate to get away and think about what had just happened.

Once her front door was closed, she dropped her keys, took off her shoes and ran barefoot down the passageway. In her tiny kitchen, like a fretful bird she picked things up, put them down, and then cupping her hands, gulped water from the tap, letting it dribble down her blouse. Haru, afraid to walk on the slippery tiles, watched her, whimpering.

'Haruko darling!' She swept the dog up into her arms and began to sway. Then to dance. Cramped, erratic Tango steps around the table. 'You are magnificent, Haru chan,' she murmured to the squirming dog. 'Magnificent.'

After dinner when Haru had settled, Megumi lingered outside Minoru's room. She slid the door open. The light from the street lamp was weak, muted by paper screens at the window. Everything was still. She could barely see the altar, let alone his portrait.

In the privacy of her bed, she luxuriated in the dance. 'You are magnificent, Mrs Yoshida.' She ran her fingers over her cheeks feeling them linger at the corners of her mouth, then brush over her lips, one hand caressing her throat, sliding to her breasts. His other hand moved down, over her stomach and she gasped. She held her breath, not wanting him to stop, listening to him saying she was beautiful and he wanted her. She had to be quiet, stifle her desire to cry out.

The following day, the heat was intense. The monsoon came closer. Megumi and Haruko sat on the sofa, staring at an empty screen. She flopped backwards, letting her cotton yukata fall open. The rain must come soon.

It came that evening, ferocious rain. Sheets of it lashed the long, narrow chain of islands, sweeping away the heat. Then, rising above the cacophony of nature, came the sound of a ringing phone.

'Hello, this is the Yoshida residence,' Megumi said.

'Kato from Dance Latin here. Am I speaking to Megumi?'

'Yes.' She grappled with the handset, trying to fix up her gaping yukata.

'Mrs Yoshida?' He spoke loudly, over the wind. 'Are you there?'

'Yes, yes. I'm here.'

'The reason I'm calling is the special package we are currently offering. I think it would suit you.'

'Oh?' She tried to remain calm, speaking so he could hear her but in a way he would find feminine and attractive. 'What kind of package?'

'We are offering a special deal. For ten lessons. It's part of our Autumn campaign. At this point, I don't believe the group class is best for you. You would benefit from some private sessions.'

Megumi's heart thumped hard against her ribs. She looked around. Somewhere Haruko was barking.

'Would I?' She paused. 'And the teacher? Who...'

'We have several very good teachers, including myself.' He laughed. 'You can nominate whomever you like. We'll work something out.'

'Yes, it sounds...'

'It would cost a little more but with your skill, Mrs Yoshida, it would be a pity not to take the opportunity.'

Megumi smiled. 'Really? It's very kind of you, but I'm sure I'm not that good.'

'Of course, you are. You are too modest. Anyway, I'll leave it with you. Don't wait too long, though. These packages are very popular.'

'Thank you. It's good of you to think of me.'

'Not at all.' He paused, cleared his throat and then said something she didn't catch. She held the handset closer but he was gone. Did he say: 'I think only of you'? Or was it: 'It's all I can think of?' It had to be something like that. Only when Haruko's wagging tail slapped her legs did she put the receiver down. The dog had pushed open the door to Minoru's room and had her late master's dried squid, still clad in soggy strips of cellophane, dangling from her mouth.

The night was filled with noises: rushing water, rattling shutters and inebriated revellers sloshing down the street. She tossed and turned, even after taking a sleeping pill. Haruko slept at the bottom of the bed, as fidgety as her mistress. Next morning, Megumi woke early, her sweaty summer nightgown twisted about her waist. She straightened herself up, then went about finding her dance clothes, a CD player, her red beret and carried them all into the formal sitting room.

'Haruko, you must stay here for a bit. I won't be long.' She closed the bedroom door so the dog couldn't follow.

Kneeling before the shrine, she tapped the singing bowl. Her hand shook and she pressed her palms together and bowed low.

'I have found my kanreki.' she said and raised her eyes.

All she wanted was for him to wish her well. But his eyes stared straight ahead and she detected no softening in the line of his lips.

What was she expecting?

She sighed and taking hold of the portrait, she laid it flat in one of the drawers under the altar. She placed the ornaments, religious utensils and food gifts, except for the squid of course, deep inside the shrine and closed the doors. It was now a small, intricately crafted wardrobe atop a chest of drawers. She glanced behind her; it felt as if someone might be watching. The room, however, was tranquil, replete with its sweet-smelling matting, dark wooden beams, white paper screens. It asked for nothing.

She got to her feet and changed into her flared dance skirt, its zip not quite at the side, her glittery top hanging awkwardly. She had forgotten her bra. In a tatami room she couldn't wear her dance shoes, any shoes. But it didn't matter. She tried on her new beret. It fitted nicely. Finally, she put on a CD and began to dance the Tango. At first, her steps were faltering but then she became more confident, and tried some pivoting and lunging.

Someone was knocking at the front door. The music must have been too loud. She bent and turned the volume down.

'Mother, are you there?'

It was Jun. He'd heard the music; she couldn't pretend to be out.

'Just a minute.' She patted her skirt, adjusted her top to no effect, and went to her front door. Jun was in the shared entrance way.

'What is it?' she called out.

'For goodness sake, Mother, open the door. I have some sake for Father.'

What could she say? The shrine's not open today? Father's having a rest. Jun would not find such a comment amusing.

'Hand it to me, Jun. I'm in the middle of cleaning. When I finish, I'll give it to Father.' She opened the door, but not too wide.

Her son stared in at her, her skew-whiff skirt, her brazen top, her saucy red cap. He pushed his glasses up his nose. Perhaps he thought that might give him a better picture.

'Mother, whatever...?'

She could see he was struggling. She was not a patient in his surgery requiring his professional advice; she was his mother. His mother of more than 30 years, standing there in front of him, he probably thought, dressed like a hostess at a dance party. As well, she was playing loud foreign music and upsetting the neighbours.

'Mother, you've been dancing,' he said in disbelief. 'Dancing right here. In front of Father.' He stared at her, shaking his head.

Poor Jun. While he tried to assess the damage, decide what to do with her, this 'fractious woman' given into his care upon the death of her husband, Megumi reached over and took hold of the sake–it was possible in his current state he might drop it.

'Thank you, Jun. I'm sure Father will be very grateful. Please come back later and drink it with him.' This would give her time to set up the shrine again after she finished her dance practice. 'We'll all have some. To celebrate his anniversary.'

Smiling at him, she began to close the door. 'Good bye now. I'll see you later.' He backed away and she pulled the latch across. It was an unthinkable act and yet she felt no shame. She wanted to laugh out loud, dance right there, just inside the door. But she restrained herself; Jun might still be outside, listening to see what she would do next. There was silence, then slow, heavy footsteps as her precious boy, her abandoned child, climbed the stairs to his own apartment. She hoped if nothing else, he would tell Kumi his mother was wearing the beret.

Back in her bedroom, Haru was lying in her basket, another abandoned child. Megumi patted the dog's head. 'A bit longer, little one and then we'll go for a walk.' She closed the door and returned to the tatami room.

'Today, we will do the Tango,' she said, extending her arm gracefully. 'Sensei, we will dance.'

Lightning Strike in Slow Motion

Thomas Hamlyn-Harris

We wake up on the western side of the range as dad swerves into a combined fruit shop and truck stop. I catch your eyes over the Christmas presents stacked between us on the back seat. We both know instinctively not to ask for an ice-block or to go to the toilet. Dad is gripping the steering wheel, his knuckles white.

'Well?' he asks without turning his head.

Drops of rain plink on the bonnet of the car and turn to steam.

'We're not going back home,' Mum says. 'It's Christm...' Mum's voice is silenced by the slam of the car door. We sit in the hot shadow of a giant fibreglass apple, while dad smokes and paces in the rain.

When I wake up again we are back on the road. A white crack of lightning punctuates the rubbery squelch of the windshield wipers as Mum turns her face to the blackening horizon. I watch her in the reflection of the passenger window. We drive for another hour to the town Mum still calls home, even though she moved to the city years ago.

We arrive at the farm and dad parks behind the packing shed. We make a dash through the heavy splats of rain to where my uncles have already started drinking on the porch. Between distracted hugs and handshakes, everyone measures the rumble of thunder in the distance. Dad takes a tinnie even though it's mid-morning. Mum opens her mouth to protest when a crash of cutlery from the kitchen silences her. She goes inside and Uncle David whistles into his tinnie, acknowledging her bravery. You purse your lips and give me a reassuring nod. We are both fluent in the silent language of adults. We sit on the porch while Grandma rages against the brooding sky by slamming kitchen cupboards.

Years later on your veranda, during a summer storm, we talk about that Christmas. How we ate cold ham with our fingers because the cutlery was hidden under the bed. You tell me Grandma hid everything metal because she believed the house would be struck by lightning. She buried the saucepans under woollen blankets and wouldn't let anyone near the stove to make a pot of tea. I was too young to remember the details or care that the gravy went unmade and the vegetables uncooked, and the weirdness of that Christmas just blurred into all the others.

You tell me that on that Christmas morning we sat for an hour while mum and dad argued in the rain. You explain that dad wanted to turn back home, not because Grandma believed in the lightning spirit but because of the drinking that followed when the storm cleared.

You remember a family that mirrored our own, on the surface at least, pulled up next to us in the shadow of the giant fibreglass apple. A girl, about your age, opened the window and called to you.

'What did you get for Christmas?' she asked, holding up a Barbie horse.

You shrugged and held up one of tightly wrapped presents that sat between us. She laughed and wound up her window. You could see the girl and her brother pointing and giggling from the back seat of their car. The rain fell and the girl danced the horse around the inside rim of the window.

There is a low rumble of thunder. You slip the cheese knife under a cushion and we both laugh. The gutters begin to overflow and you speak softly as if addressing the rain.

'I thought when we finally opened our Christmas presents I would get the same Barbie horse,' you say, blushing at the hold the memory still has over you.

'I've never heard the Barbie horse story before' I say, making a mental note to buy your daughter one for Christmas.

'It's not a story,' you say, 'it's just a memory... it doesn't mean anything.'

I see you're struggling but I can't let this moment pass without digging a little deeper.

'Do you remember mum's cat-in-the-suitcase story?' I ask.

'Are you going to bring this up again?' you say.

'She packed her cat into a small suitcase and ran away from home when she was five. She dragged a suitcase with a fluffy tail through barbed wire fences and across cow paddocks to the neighbour's house. And when they took her home no one had noticed she was gone. She tells it like a fond childhood memory of cats, the punchline being how high it jumped when she finally opened the lid.'

You smile at my retelling. Perhaps I have embellished it.

'It's not just a story,' I say, 'What was she running from?'

Your daughter calls from the bedroom and you get up to help her into her pyjamas. Your hand on my shoulder tells me the conversation is over.

I can hear you in the kitchen now, gently opening and closing cupboard doors, preparing dinner. I watch the storm and wish we had better words for second-hand memories, words better suited to how time gathers and oscillates, a way to describe the echo of silence that recurs over generations.

I wish there was a way to tell you I am not afraid anymore.

Sean

Judi Morison

Eve shared the Kiama station waiting room with a middle-aged hippie couple who reeked of pot, and a young tradie in a high-vis vest. He had fair, curly hair, just like her boy Sean. She felt the three pairs of eyes on her and pulled her blue vinyl shopping trolley closer, tucking her red-and-white-checked storage bag behind her legs. She'd paid four dollars for it at Big W but it looked a bit worse for wear—the zip broken from cramming her clothes in, the handles just holding on.

The trolley was sturdier. Just right for carrying her big black umbrella. She'd found the brolly after a storm—blown inside out, with a bent spoke—but it kept off most of the rain. The trolley was perfect for stowing a cask of port too, or a couple of bottles if she could pick them up cheap. She reached in and patted the paper bag containing a bottle of McWilliam's Tawny she'd bought for less than three dollars at Dan Murphy's—cheaper than a cask.

The doors of the 2.39 am to Sydney slid open and Eve hauled her trolley into a quiet carriage. She had to get some sleep. With a bit of luck she could nab two hours before Central. The blue-and-yellow velour seats were hard but not too bad once she'd curled into the three-seater at the back of the downstairs carriage, under the stairs. She jammed her trolley and bag between the seats, took a swig from her bottle before re-burying it, and covered herself with the thick man's overcoat she'd found at Vinnies in Surry Hills. The girl had let her have it for five dollars.

Forty minutes later, Eve woke to singing. Icy air whipped through the open doors. Wollongong. A crowd of young blokes getting on, heading home to their soft beds in the suburbs. Even from downstairs she could smell the beer on them as they slurred, not in unison, 'in the paaaalm of his haaands'.

'Shut up!' she shouted. 'I'm trying to get some sleep. It's a *quiet* carriage, for fuck's sake.'

The young blokes swarmed down the steps and stood in the aisle, laughing at her. Then they started in with 'She's a piss-pot through and through'.

After working behind a bar for over forty years, Eve knew all about drunken louts. She'd learned to deal with their bloody cheek, their need to show how tough they were, by having a go at a woman. In the old days she'd given them as good as she got, and she could still do it.

'Geez, you lot must have tiny todgers,' she said after the first verse, 'if you need to prove yourselves so bad.'

Older men in the pubs used to pull up young blokes when they got out of hand. Couldn't count on that any more though, not on the trains. Things had changed. For one, she wasn't young any more. She'd been a looker in her day—a few blokes had told her so—but where'd that got her? Married at twenty to Martin. Swept her off her feet, he had. No other blokes ever bought her flowers or asked her what she'd like to see at the flicks. Martin took her to proper restaurants too, not just some greasy spoon. And in bed—she shivered thinking about that. 'You're the love of my life,' he'd whispered, and she'd said it straight back to him. But that hadn't turned out so shit hot.

She hadn't shut those ratbags up either, and the other three passengers in the carriage didn't look like they'd be much help if things turned nasty. Should've kept her trap shut.

The mongrels kept it up, hanging over the seat in front of her, grabbing at her bag. She pulled out her brolly to defend herself but, as the train pulled into Bulli, the loudest one snatched it and threw it down the aisle. Then they all clomped up the stairs, still singing their stupid song.

'Fucking cheeky bastards,' she grumbled, getting up to fetch the brolly. She took another sweet swig before she settled down again. Her Sean would never carry on like that. He was a quiet boy, gentle.

At Central, she was rushing to make the turnaround, to jump the next train down the coast. Six minutes to scuttle up and across from platform 24, in the dank bowels of the station, to the country platforms. The 5.19 am to Kiama wouldn't have many passengers: the odd early bird on holiday, a few tradies heading south to work. And a handful like her, looking for a safe spot to put their heads down for a couple of hours before the trains became a no-go area, patrolled by railway police.

Pushing her trolley off the escalator onto the concourse, she was pulled up short by a sign: *Derailment on South Coast Line. Buses Operate Between Central and Kiama.* What the fuck? Bleary-eyed from too little sleep and half a bottle of port, she followed the arrows pointing to the street.

The August wind needled through the terminal and lights blazing inside the vaulted sandstone cavern intensified the blackness outside. An icy gust hit her as she passed through the archway onto the drive, where a straggle of passengers waited at the coach bay.

She slid the brown paper bag out of her shopping trolley, stole a quick slug for warmth, and slipped the bottle into her deep overcoat pocket. They'd stick the trolley in the luggage hold—if they let her on. But why did she want to get on anyway? They'd make her wear a seat-belt, wouldn't let her lie down. No chance of sleep.

Her palms were sweaty, her stomach knotted. Where to go? Suburban trains weren't safe. Too many psychos around, with all the ice. She shivered. She couldn't hang around outside the terminal like the old bloke on the doorstep, his only defence against the freezing sandstone and dawn chill a thin sleeping bag and gutful of grog.

The coach to Kiama pulled in and stood idling like a panting beast, belching diesel fumes. A swarm of uniformed men with clipboards surrounded it. Eve's eyes darted from the coach to the terminal and back again. She couldn't decide. Like when she fell pregnant with Sean. She hadn't known what to do then. She'd made all sorts of plans in her head, but Martin's cries of 'I'm no bloody use to you!' were getting more frequent, and she knew she couldn't look after him and a baby as well. I can't keep it, she eventually told herself. But she was already sixteen weeks gone by then, so she'd had her curly-haired boy.

The drawn-out croak of an ibis drifted up from Belmore Park. Hang around there till the food van came? When was that? What day was it, anyway? Weekend? Weekday?

The dossers in the handful of tents that had sprung up again in the park had it good. Their camps looked cosy, tucked under the shelter of the fig and plane trees. Once, one of the tent people had called her over as she walked through the park. 'Come and have a yarn, darl,' he'd said, holding up a bottle. But she'd always kept her distance from the park people.

She'd been tempted though. It was a while since she'd had male company. After Martin had gone, she'd moved away from Coogee, where they'd sunbaked and swum together on their days off. She'd rented a little flat in down-at-heel Enmore and got on with her life, working behind the bar in pubs and clubs around Newtown. A few nips of vodka before she went in to work and she'd sail through her shift. And after closing, there was always a drink on offer from one of the punters who'd drooled over her cleavage all night. It was one bloke after another, taking what they wanted and moving on. She never let it worry her, though. She'd played them too, closing her eyes and imagining Martin's lips and hands on her body.

No, she couldn't risk the park till light. Maybe she could have a bit of a lie-down in the station. She'd need a few more pulls on her bottle to face the stinking tiled floor. But one of the black-and-orange uniforms would only shake her awake and move her on. It'd have to be the coach.

She touched the familiar shape in her coat pocket for luck and, holding tight to her bag, dragged her trolley to the coach bay. Keeping her eyes down, she parked it in front of the hold, where the driver was loading up a stroller and suitcase. She was just about to heave herself onto the step of the coach when the boss cocky stepped in front of her.

'Where do you think you're going, love?' he asked, thrusting his belly and clipboard against her, knocking her bag from her shaking hands.

She couldn't think what to say. Passengers were gawping from the coach windows and a group of Asian tourists scurrying towards the terminal slowed and stared.

'No drinking on City Rail. And the driver doesn't want your lice-ridden bag on his bus either. Now hop it, there's a good girl.'

The shame of it! Just like after she had Sean, facing the neighbours and local shopkeepers, who'd watched her belly swell and seemed to have an investment in the growing life.

She saw the questions in their eyes when she came home from hospital. Some of the women stopped her on the streets, asking 'Where's the little one?' She'd lied, mumbled something about Sean's lungs not being properly developed.

But her body couldn't lie. Curled up on the loungeroom floor, her stomach heaving, she felt like her womb was trying to draw Sean back. And when her swollen breasts leaked, despite the medicine they'd given her to dry them up, she could hardly bear it. That milk should have been making her Sean strong.

What could she tell the neighbours? Martin kept to himself and hadn't let on to anyone else how crook he was—or that the doctors said he would only get worse. His eyes had gone first. Everything blurred, until he couldn't work any more. Then his words got messed up. Neighbours must've thought he was pissed all the time. His legs started to go on him six months into her pregnancy.

'Bloody MS!' he said, counting out the tablets that never did any good. 'What sort of man have you saddled yourself with?'

'We're a team, you and me,' she said, as she cut up the meals he couldn't see clearly, got him safely to his doctor's appointments, cheered him on with his exercises and helped him up when he tripped over his drop foot, or his legs went spastic. She could hardly make out the mangled words he whispered in bed, and words were all he could manage. She couldn't have cared for him and Sean as well.

'I'm no bloody use to you at all,' he'd said, when his bladder went haywire, and when things got worse. 'The MS Society can put me in a nursing home. You can get on with your life, forget about me.'

'Teamwork, remember!' she'd said. 'We can manage together.'

They did too, for a while. And when she had to admit that she couldn't look after him any more—she couldn't lift him—the only choice was that bloody awful nursing home, with old codgers dying all around. She still spent most of every day there with him, making sure he ate. The staff didn't have time to feed him when he couldn't lift a knife or fork. She'd feed him, then rub cream into his cramping feet, cut his fingernails. She'd try to get him laughing with stories about the odd characters at the pub but he'd say 'Go home and get some rest,' or 'Get out and have some fun.' She'd only leave him to work her night shift at the Coogee Bay, though. Then, heading home to the empty flat in the early hours, she'd think about Sean, asleep in his bed, somewhere, and pray he wasn't lonely.

She could never forget her Sean, even though she only saw him twice, the first time when she held him after his birth. Her palm cradled his tiny head, her hand making a nest for it as she traced a memory with her fingertips and wound his wispy golden curls around her little finger.

They brought the papers for her to sign on day three. The surge of milk to her swollen breasts had caught her by surprise. Still exhausted from the birth, she lay on her side, curled up like a foetus herself, her breasts aching, heavy womb cramping, and barb-like stitches nagging.

'Are you sure you're making the right decision?' the matron asked, rousing her to hand her the pen. She listened to the soft ticking sound of the bub nursing in the bed beside her, felt her own milk leak and pool in the folds of her crumpled nightie. She almost changed her mind.

But Martin needed her more than Sean did. The social worker let her hold him once more, to say goodbye. He was perfect. Blueish eyes, ivory skin, button nose. All the nurses said what a thick head of hair he had, how special his curls were.

'They'll find you another mum who'll look after you, and she'll love you almost as much as I do,' she told him.

Her fingers caressed every tiny part of him. She nuzzled his silky hair and covered his tummy with butterfly kisses. And he was good as gold, her Sean, not a peep out of him. She hadn't stopped crying for weeks.

But Martin had been the love of her life. And when he couldn't swallow the food she spooned into his mouth, and his lungs stopped working, she'd had to let him go too. Her punishment for giving up Sean.

She would've given anything to hang onto them both. And she'd never managed to get herself pregnant again, for all the blokes she screwed. But ever since Martin died she'd been trying to make up for it, to find Sean. The Salvos showed her the ropes but there was a lot of paperwork to fill in. She'd never been much good at that sort of thing, and since she'd lost her flat she didn't have an address for anyone to contact her by mail.

Still, she never stopped looking. Sometimes she thought she'd found Sean, but mums got angry when she touched their little ones' golden curls. They'd get up in a huff and move to another seat in the train or bus when she sat beside them.

A copper caught her talking to a fair-haired toddler that some mother had left in a stroller parked outside the newsagent.

'Keep your dirty hands off other people's kiddies,' he shouted, his red face too close to hers, 'or I'll have to pull you in.' She'd only been asking the little one's name.

Young blokes could turn turn nasty too, when she chased after them to have a better look at their blue eyes.

'I'm not fuckin Sean,' one fair-haired bloke had shouted in her face, flecking her with spit before he pushed her out of the way.

'Get a life, ya derro,' another curly-haired young fella had yelled at her, kicking over her trolley and smashing a full bottle of Tawny.

And once people looked at you like you were worthless, and you'd bargained away your child to hang onto the man you loved, you had to admit they were right.

She stood at the bottom of the coach steps, paralysed, for what must have been ages until, from behind the idling coach, a figure slid into view like a phantom. She recognised him, a scrawny-looking young bloke, with dark, spiky hair. She'd seen him around Eddy Avenue before, quick to find a few coins for the beggars camped in the colonnade outside the 7-Eleven. She'd seen him late at night, too. Shickered. Stumbling along Enmore Road or King Street, well after the pubs and bars had closed, his eyes filled with his own brand of pain.

Now he shouldered her bag, grabbed her trolley, and took her by the elbow at the same time. 'C'mon Aunty,' he said, striding out, leading her back towards the terminal. 'We can make the Newcastle train if we're quick.'

She raised her eyes to look at him. Up close, he was a lot like her Sean.

Kembo is Home

Chemutai Glasheen

'*Mwenda! Chokora! Kicha!*'

The taunting was relentless. Someone hit him in the back of the head and the force of it knocked Kembo flat. He landed on his face, on the dusty tarmac bleached grey in the sun. His body recoiled from the searing heat. He gulped for air but instead his lungs filled with scorching air. He could taste something salty in his mouth and knew it was blood. He had become familiar with the taste. He did not dare look up. He knew the pair of boots, inches from his face, belonged to Jim. More boys stood around in a circle laughing and yelling. He fixed his eyes on the cracks in the tarmac. He ran his tongue on the inside of his mouth. No broken teeth. He hoped that if he did not say a word, if he did not move, the boys would all eventually get bored and go away.

'Get up, you chicken!'

'Stand up and fight for yourself!'

Kembo still didn't look up. Eventually, the crowd of bullies left. Kembo spat out the blood which had collected in his mouth, blew his nose with his right hand, and wiped his fingers on the ground. He struggled to his feet. A surge of pain hit him in the shin. He held still and waited for it to abate. He patted himself down and noted with dismay that his only good pair of trousers had ripped down the front to reveal what was left of the threads that once held together as underwear. Clutching his shirt where he had lost a couple of buttons and picking up his bag, he dragged himself home. His body ached but deep inside of him was another pain. It was always there with him, even after his bruises healed. He fought back tears. He was not a kid anymore. But his tears refused to be quelled.

'Mama,' he called as he limped through the door.

'Mama,' he called again.

Kembo was not expecting an answer. He carefully placed the plastic bag, which contained the only two exercise books he owned, in the corner of the room. They had been given to him by Mrs Omollo, his English teacher. He used them for every single subject. He had trained himself to write in small writing and on every available space so his books would last the entire term.

His eyes swept around the tiny room he shared with his mother. She was seated on the mattress on the floor in the corner, running her fingers up and down the wall. She was muttering to herself as usual, but Kembo noticed that the *matutas* on her head were neatly done. Winnie, from the salon two doors away, must have had some spare time—she did Mama's hair whenever she could. He liked it when Mama's hair was done. It made her look like a mother.

Kembo walked over and knelt beside her to straighten her skirt. Then he used the edge of her *lesso* to wipe the drool from the corner of her mouth. He took her by the hands and said to her 'Kembo is home.'

'Kembo is home. Kembo is home,' she repeated to herself.

Mama's eyes were still pinned to the wall even though Kembo held her face toward him. He waited patiently for her eye movements to focus on him. When they did, it was for just a fleeting moment, a brief smile, before she turned back to the wall. He buried his face in her hands for a moment. Mama's hands were soft. Clean and soft. Too soft. How different life would have been, had she the ashy grey and calloused hands of the many women who broke stones all day in the quarry!

'How was your day?' he asked her, again not expecting a response. His mother continued running her fingers up and down the cement wall.

'Kembo is home,' she was saying.

'School was fine,' he lied to her. 'Everybody is so nice and so helpful.' He swallowed hard and slumped onto the mattress. He longed to close his eyes and shut out the day but there was too much to do. He shook off the sleep, and got to his feet, his jaw clenched.

'The *githeri* is ready and we should eat soon,' he said, not waiting for a reply. 'Sorry, today we will eat it cold.'

He set about dishing the *githeri* he had cooked a few days ago into two bowls. He noticed his mother was fidgeting and so he promptly stopped what he was doing and went and took her hand.

He helped her stand up and led her out to the courtyard towards the toilets.

'Come on Mama,' he encouraged.

Mama Njoki was fanning her *jiko*, and, when she saw them, she quickly came over and took Mama's hand. The neighbours knew

Kembo by name and they had taken it upon themselves to keep an eye on both him and his mother.

'Let me help her, okay?'

Kembo gratefully accepted Mama Njoki's help. He had been attending to his mother as long as he could remember. He never considered it strange to take his mother to the toilet or the bathroom. He was familiar with his mother's nakedness.

'*Asante sana,*' he murmured his thanks.

Kembo bent to pick up an empty *blueband* sachet. The stones he had swept to the corner were back on the pavement, obviously left there by the children who were playing *banta*. He was slightly irritated by them, envying the kids their ability to play late into the evening. The last time he joined in, they played till night fell and his mother went to bed without dinner. He picked up one of the pebbles and held it for a while. *Tho!* He didn't need to play childish games anymore! He twitched to hurl it across the compound but instead, he flicked it back onto the pavement. The courtyard was relatively clean. He swept it every morning before he left for school. Mzee Ishmael, the landlord, had agreed to have him clean all the shared spaces, including the bathrooms and toilets, in exchange for the single room he shared with his mother.

There were eight houses that opened onto the courtyard. They all looked alike. The light blue paint on the window frames and doors looked like dried blisters one couldn't resist peeling. The cement on the walkway had cracks and holes through which weeds consistently pushed. To the right, across from his room, a large *mabati* was held in place by a post to serve as a gate. From the block behind them came endless shrieks of carefree children. Someone was cooking *chapati*. A family would later be sitting on the floor, pulling each one apart, sharing it around and inhaling the smoke infused warmth. He shook off the twist in his stomach and focused his eyes on a neighbour pushing through the gate, bowed low with a sack of potatoes on his back, in readiness for market day later in the week.

Kembo walked back to the house. When Mama Njoki arrived with his mother, she informed him that Mama Jimi had been looking for him a little earlier. He liked Mama Jimi. He knew she needed help around the house, and usually he worked for her on the weekend, cleaning or weeding the garden. She paid him about two hundred shillings, which was generous. Many times, she would also pack him some food or some old clothes for both him and his mother.

'*Asante* Mama Njoki, thank you very much,' he said quietly. 'I will try to see her soon.'

'Take care of Mama,' she said. 'Remember, call me if you need anything.'

'Thank you once again,' he responded, as he straightened Mama's blanket.

'Sit Mama Kembo,' Mama Njoki said as she settled his mother on the blanket before she left.

'Here is food, Mama,' he put the *githeri* in front of his mother. 'I need to go see Mama Jimi before it gets dark. I won't be long and Mama Njoki will be just outside the door,' he reassured her.

What did Mama Jimi want? This was a Wednesday. She usually insisted that he focus on his homework during the week.

Mama Jimi lived about ten minutes away. He tried to jog but his shin screamed from the kicks he had received earlier. He gritted his teeth. Just one more step, one more. He willed himself to acknowledge those he passed, with a polite smile. His mind was on school, on the two more years he had left.

He enjoyed learning and he particularly liked Mrs Omollo. She was patient with him and didn't yell at him when he didn't have a book. He loved the way she always said, 'Give it a try, nothing is easy the first time'. Whenever she asked him a question, she would move around the room, so she was always between him and the bulging eyes of the bullies. He wanted to work hard for her. Unlike some teachers, she never encouraged him to stay home and look after his mother, or asked him simple questions and then declared 'I really admire you.'

Kembo wanted to stay in school and he needed money for his tuition. He arrived at Mama Jimi's house in a lot of pain, and the door opened just as he raised his hand to knock. Kembo almost keeled over at the sight of the person who opened the door.

'I... I'm...' his voice trailed off.

'What do you want?' thundered Jim, the bully from school.

'I'm... sorry.' Kembo closed his eyes and braced himself for the blow that he expected would follow.

'Is that Kembo at the door?' Mama Jimi called from inside.

'Eh... are you Kembo?' Jimi seemed just as taken aback as Kembo was. He turned and yelled, 'You mean this is the Kembo with the mad mother?'

'Eish!' His mother's voice was sharp as she nudged her son out of the way. She lowered her voice to speak to her son but Kembo could hear her.

'We don't say that. She has an illness of the brain. Some sort of intellectual disability, they call it.'

Jim swallowed and kept his head down.

'Come in Kembo,' He heard her say. 'This is my son, Jim. You probably don't know each other but he goes to the same school as you. He is in the higher class.'

She paused and looked a little puzzled at the two boys, who could not hide that they recognised each other.

'Come in, come in,' she urged.

Mama Jimi always said her son was away at football training, trying to be the next Samuel Eto'o. Out of the corner of his eye, Kembo caught sight of Jim beckoning his mother to go into the next room. They closed the door behind them.

Kembo looked around wondering whether he should start cleaning, like he did on Saturdays, or wait for instructions from Mama Jimi. To think she was Jim's mother! And that Jim was in the next room! He shuddered and shifted his weight to the other foot only to be jerked back in pain. He held his breath. He reached down to rub his shin which had become the sweet spot for Jim's football drills. He looked around for something to lean on. He tried to lean on the sofa but straightened up right away. He took a step back and rested against the wall instead. His mind was racing. He tried to keep his breathing even. He wiped his hands on his shorts and hoped Mama Jimi wouldn't see him hobbling. How would he explain it?

When the door opened, he took a quick step towards Mama Jimi.

'Yes, Mama Jimi?' He asked, clasping his hands.

'I've got guests tomorrow,' Mama Jimi said. 'I need to have these floors scrubbed thoroughly. You know where everything is, don't you?'

'Yes, Mama Jimi,' he replied.

Kembo picked up the red bucket from behind the kitchen cupboard. He half-filled it with water and sprinkled a little soap on the sitting room floor. He went back to the kitchen for the old towel with which to dry off the water once he had finished scrubbing.

Kembo crouched on the floor with a brush in his hands, glad that he had something to keep them from trembling. He scrubbed harder than usual, and he was busy working when two familiar feet stood in front of him. Instinctively, he covered his head with his hands and shut his eyes tight. He held his breath.

'Here, I brought you another towel,' said Jim, and dropped it on Kembo's head.

Kembo didn't respond. He waited a little longer before opening his eyes. He shook the towel off and fixed his wary gaze on Jim's feet. He heard Mama Jimi come into the room.

'Brush for you, Jim,' she said.

'What? Why do I have to clean?' Jim asked.

'We have just spoken about this. It would be nice for you to start doing more around the house. Get on with it.'

'Isn't that what you are paying him to do? This is so unfair!' Jim's voice was little high, which surprised Kembo.

'Your choice, you can either help out now or miss football on Saturday.'

Kembo kept his head down during the entire exchange. Slowly, he relaxed his grip on the scrubbing brush. A tiny smile touched his lips. Someone could make Jim do something he did not want to do!

'I am not scrubbing! I will only dry,' and with that Jim grabbed the towel he had dropped on Kembo moments ago and got to work in the corner.

Mama Jimi watched them for a while, and, with a slight smile at Kembo, she left the sitting room.

They worked in silence. Kembo scrubbing. Jim drying. When Jim ran his towel over the parts that Kembo hadn't scrubbed, Kembo said nothing. He went over the spot.

'What are you doing?' Jim sounded a little angry.

'Your mother wants every spot scrubbed,' Kembo said simply.

'So why didn't you tell me you hadn't scrubbed that end?'

Kembo didn't answer but shrugged his shoulders instead, loosening his muscles a little.

'Huh? You really need to learn to speak up. You have a voice, use it.' Jim sounded a little irritated.

'That bit is done,' Kembo said, and turned away to begin working backwards from the door towards the centre of the room. He took his time cleaning the grout lines on the tile floor. Then he shuffled backwards, bumping into Jim, who went tumbling into the bucket of water and onto the floor.

'*Shenzi!*' Jim swore out loud.

'Sorry. I'm so sorry,' Kembo said, over and over, while reaching for Jim's arm to help him up.

'I can get myself up,' snapped Jim.

'I really didn't mean to... I didn't see you.'

'How many sorrys?' Jim raised himself up to a sitting position. 'Is that a record?'

Kembo was confused. Jim hadn't raised his voice or called him names. He had an odd look on his face and Kembo looked away, unsure what to expect.

'Bravo Kembo, you finally knocked me down! We are now even.'

Was that a smile at the corner of Jim's mouth? Kembo was really confused. He didn't respond.

'Here, help me up now,' Jim said, his arm outstretched.

Kembo took it but he didn't have to do much as Jim pushed himself onto his feet. Jim towered over him with a quizzical look in his eyes.

'You are only little, aren't you?' Jim finally said.

I am the same one you squash daily, Kembo thought.

'Let's finish up here,' Jim said and picked up his towel. There was something new about the way Jim spoke to him. The usual venom wasn't there. They worked in silence until the work was done. Mama Jimi appeared at the door. If she noticed anything unusual about the two, she never said a thing.

'Thank you so much Kembo. My back doesn't allow me to clean floors and so I am extra grateful to you. Thank you again.'

Kembo thanked her too, with a slight bow and with his hands pressed together.

'I will pay you on the weekend, Kembo, I hope that is okay with you,' she added. 'But here, take this home to your mother.' Mama Jimi put a plastic bag in Kembo's hand.

'You better hurry up, you must have homework.'

Kembo thanked her once again and turned to walk home.

'Kembo,' Jim called out to him.

What! No *kicha* or *chokora*. Just his name. It sounded strange hearing his name uttered by Jim.

Kembo stopped and waited, unsure what to expect. Jim ran up to him.

'About school...' he hesitated, 'it will never happen again. No one will touch you. I'll make sure of that.'

Kembo wasn't sure how to respond, so he kept it simple. 'Okay.'

'Goodbye,' Jim said, 'and *maze*, I'm sorry.' He said this softly, rubbing the nape of his neck. 'I don't know why I do it. Maybe just because I can.'

'Okay,' Kembo said again, and this time he managed a weak smile.

He turned and made his way home. As he walked away, he glanced into the bag to see what Mama Jimi had packed for him. It was a *lesso* and a blanket. Mother would love it, he thought, as he reached in to feel the blanket. He also touched something wrapped in plastic. He drew it out quickly and stopped still, staring at a pair of new black and red striped underwear. New undies! With shaking hands, he peeled off the wrapping and then brought them to his nose. He drank in the newness of them. As he inhaled a second time, he couldn't help tearing up. He quickened his pace home, his step lighter, the ache in his shin dull.

Youngbloods

Carly Rawson

These days Bonnie was strictly forward facing. She paid good money for psychological instruction and adhered to it like a devotee. Five mornings a week she was dragged from the city's bowels by an escalator so steep that she felt herself trapped in a free-falling dream. Each morning she grit her teeth against it and focused on her breathing. She read and reread the safety signs. *Be safe! Hold on and refrain from looking behind or below you.* These were words to live by.

She hadn't thought about him in years. Not really. Then something changed. She started seeing him everywhere. Leaning against walls. Stumbling across the street. Men whose prison time had become muscle memory, clenching their fists shut and pulling their jaws tight like wire. Men with too short hair and brand new shoes. Young men full of old anger. She would see them and feel the sudden catch, an erotic charge, like the flare of a pilot flame, and she'd hurry past without meeting their eyes.

She fell off a cliff and he caught her. It was late and the sea was alive with microscopic animal light that flashed like blue lightning as it broke against the shore. Watching from the Rotary park lookout she was drawn over the railing by voices rising from the darkness. She slipped, skimming down shale, grasping at air, the ocean cold and hard beneath her, and he stepped out of his hut for a piss and pulled her in. She was drunk. When she woke the next morning, she was surprised to find herself in her own bed. She surveyed the damage—nine broken nails, gravel studded beneath the skin of her stomach, and a fugitive boyfriend.

His name was Jay. He was twenty years old. He had a rap sheet a mile long, a reputation of mythical proportions. Everyone had a story. He was a mad dog. A sadist. A psychopath. Raised out in the backblocks where the forest crowded the fence line and machinery lay rusting among the ruined cars and tin sheds. Mentally rearranged by a stepfather who chained him to the dog kennel for days on end, shooting at him when he tried to escape. Or was it his mother who was tethered... It all depends on who was doing the telling. Someone was running, someone had a gun, and someone was tied to a kennel. The only indisputable fact, cast aside as an immovable truth and of no service to anyone, was that he had been there. She thought he was beautiful. His strange green eyes always wide open. He looked constantly startled, ever-alert, like the Afghan girl on the cover of the old National Geographic in the doctor's surgery. She knew Jay was trouble of a serious kind, but he was her first chance at a boyfriend and she was longing to be touched.

The town was slowly withering. There were too few reasons to live there and many more to leave. Even the tourists gave it a wide berth. It was the wrong kind of rugged, too wild. The people were hostile. The jobs were gone—the cannery had moved offshore and the fish stocks were drying up, leaving trawlers docked five-a-breast down at the wharf. Gossip passed the time, fuelling spot fires that burned until the pension checks came in and drunken goodwill surged through the streets like a spring tide. It was brutal stuff but like sport, or war, there were rules of engagement. The latest rumours surrounding Jay felt different, quietly dangerous, and Bonnie had no idea of what to do but step over them like broken glass in the sand.

Jay lived with his mother and sister in a commission house. His sister Ruby had cystic fibrosis. His mother sold speed. Bonnie met her once, a whippet of a woman with a face like a blade. The deference she directed towards her son was underpinned with fear or apology or both. Bonnie watched her fret as she brewed the tea, fumbling as she topped up his cigarette packet from her own. She knew that some of what she'd heard must have been true.

There were things she could personally vouch for: he hated the cops, he loved his mum, and he deified his sister. Ruby's slow suffocation, he told her, made him want to punch a hole in the world. They were sitting on his bed and a hacking cough started up across the hall as if on cue. She couldn't look him in the eye. His room was spotless and unadorned except for a Romper Stomper poster and a serious looking crossbow in the corner. He had very pale skin and girlish auburn curls. His clothes and hair were fragrantly clean, a heady mix of Omo and synthetic apricot. She wondered how he kept the bush off him—the others reeked of bongwater and wet wool—they were covered in mud and mosquito bites, scabs and bruises. When he reached for her his grip was light. They sat together quietly stoned, watching the dust turn in the air. She stroked his wrist, smoothing welts of scar tissue beneath her thumb.

She found a new life through truancy. Squeezing between the demountable classrooms at recess and running full pelt across the back paddock. She never felt as purposeful as she did when she was running towards him. Her flannel shirt full of wind, her body shuddering with adrenaline like a bolting horse. Rage-Against-The-Machine looping through her head, feet pounding the earth, dirt flinging from her heels. They always waited for her by the barbed-wire fence, half hidden in the scrub like a bush militia. Jay, his two lieutenants, Ozzie and Ryan, and Sam, their twelve-year-old scout. They never referred to themselves that way, and nor did he, but the hierarchy was clear. Beans had been the equalizer but he was gone and they never spoke about him, the effort to keep it at bay almost silencing them completely.

They avoided roads. Jay headed up the line and everyone fell in behind him. Someone was always shouldering a slab of beer as they snaked their way through derelict backyards, caravan parks, around the stinking edge of the lake, the mud sucking at their boots, along fire trails, dirt bike tracks, and finally into the maw of the bush. Dead quiet except for the occasional flick of a lighter and the *clink clink clink* of the beers in the box. Turn around, look for me, look at me—she pleaded with the back of his head, but he never looked back, not once.

They robbed local shops and ripped crops of weed, spending their days rotating their loot between hideouts. Their lives were like a boys-own-adventure repurposed for criminals. They had stashes in burnt out cars and in bark humpies, in ply-board shacks and in caves beneath dripping, fern covered escarpments. None of them had a job and they worked hard to keep it that way. They'd built a clubhouse of sorts, a place they called The Hut, and it was their pride and joy. It had taken months to excavate it into the cliffside, countless midnight raids on works sites for timber to reinforce the earthen walls. It was remarkable engineering, so improbable that it safeguarded them against both the cops and vigilante locals. She liked it there, the way their faces and limbs loosened, how they laughed when the wind blew seawards, taking the sound with it.

The smoke in the hut was so compressed it had a weight of its own—it reminded her of swimming into a bloom of jellyfish, the weird dread she felt with all that alien flesh jostling against her. Starved of air, she pushed through the thick canvas door and found Sam crouched on the ledge, keeping watch. The swell sounded like cars crashing as it broke against the rocks below them. He looked at her and bent to pick up a stone, throwing it down into the darkness. 'That could have been you.'

'Yeh.'

'But he caught you, hey?'

She nodded, breathing deeply.

He pointed to the left of the headland. 'See over there? That rocky bit with the she-oak? That's where Beans fell.'

'I thought he jumped.'

Sam shrugged and turned away, wiping his nose on the sleeve of his hoody. 'They've been saying that Jay threw him. Did you know that?'

'Yeh.'

He stood up and shook out his legs. Light bled out through the gaps in the ply and when he turned to her, he looked very young and afraid.

'You're all fucked,' he said and hoisted himself up the cliff and into the night.

The bush made her paranoid. The weed made her paranoid. She was always smoking weed in the bush. The boys never stopped pacing, as taut and electrified as Dobermans. Things thrashed through the undergrowth. She couldn't distinguish between their fears and her own.

They were hemmed in on three sides by trees, a small town teetering on the edge of the ocean. Everyone, at least once, had climbed a fence or beaten through the bush in search of something up on the cliffs. Sitting there, looking out at the clean, empty air you could imagine yourself free of whatever it was that had brought you there. Beans was dead but so were scores of others—country boys, dying in car accidents, on football fields, trapped in the cabins of sinking trawlers, hanging from the eaves of their father's sheds, flying off cliffs or being thrown. She imagined Beans fell after a scuffle. An accident. She didn't imagine that he had been alone.

She was no longer an invisible little girl. Into the town's overactive imagination she emerged, centrestage, unrehearsed and with a ready-made reputation. She was Jay's girl and fair game for gossip and unsolicited advice. 'If you're seeing my nephew, you're stupider than I gave you credit for,' her English teacher said to her in the hall.

'Stay away from him. I've heard he's not right in the head,' her mother said, reaching for her wine as she stroked the hairy thigh of her new girlfriend.

'Ryan's gone. Left town. He had a fight with Jay and afterwards he found shards of glass in his beer,' her best friend said, breathless with excitement at her door.

Ozzie found her in the chicken shop. 'There's a lot of fellas coming down from up the coast this weekend. Going to get pretty rowdy, you might want to steer clear.' He eyed the chips in the Bain Marie. 'Bonn. You might want to steer clear, ya know, in general,' he said.

'If you break up with me, I'll take the crossbow down to the station and let the pigs finish me off,' Jay said.

Jay called—said he was coming over. She had never spoken to him on the phone and he'd never been to her house. She lived on a main road—there were no back ways, no way of not being seen. She knew he wasn't coming over for a cup of tea. She didn't know what to do. She showered, spread herself apart and smelt herself and showered again. He arrived and they went to her room. She burned with shame on her single bed, it's girlish floral spread. He lay his weight on her, his hands beneath him scratching at the buttons of her shirt. There wasn't enough room in her mouth for his tongue. He ground himself against her leg and she wondered what action was required of her. She searched her body for some sign of readiness but there were none. Feeling small and scared she raised a hand to his shoulder and pushed back. To her surprise, he stopped. Rolled off her and swung his legs into his boots. Turned away from her as he slid a hand beneath his belt and shifted his swollen cock to a less conspicuous position. He bent down, brushing the hair from her face and kissing both her eyes. And then he was standing at the door, telling her it was okay like he meant it. She watched him walk away along the wide-open road, the afternoon sun shining on his clean hair and thought she might love him. And then the police pulled him from his bed in the middle of the night and he was gone.

The last time she saw him was at a party. She heard her name called from somewhere outside the spill of noise and lights.

'Bonnie. Bonnie, come 'ere.'

He was alone, sitting hunched on the low brick fence, his back to the party.

'How you been, Bonn?'

'Alright. You?'

'I've been locked up. Just got out.'

'Yeah, I heard.'

'Yeah? What else have you heard?'

Her skin prickled. Someone had spread a rumour that he'd been caught fucking his neighbour's sheep. The story got filthier, the further it was passed down the line. He'd been gone too long and they'd turned, punishing him for the shame of having served him.

'I haven't heard much. Been keeping my head down. You know, school and all.'

She looked back over her shoulder at the party but it had folded in upon itself like a fist. He lit a cigarette and in the brief flare of light she saw that his curls were gone, noted the ugly seam of shiny purple skin raised by crude stitching above his eyebrow.

'You scared of me, Bonn?' he said, his voice low and hopeful.

She could smell him in the dark, his clean clothes and his prison tobacco. She was tired of all of it.

'Nah.'

He laughed and stood up.

'Good girl,' he said, pulling his hood down over his eyes and disappearing into the shadows.

She left town not long after. She'd been pushing against the threshold of her own bad behaviour trying to find a way through. It didn't take long. She was kicked out of school first and then home. Two doors in two days. The mill was laying off workers and a trawler had gone down with its' crew. People were looking inwards to their own trouble—they had no time for hers. She moved to the city where she imagined things would be different, less savage. She was young, green and alone, and cruelly mistaken. She thought of him often during those first few years, in the mornings when the door shut behind another man who had stayed only long enough to empty himself. She remembered the warm sun in her room and how he stopped at the touch of her hand, a thief confronted with the only thing he wouldn't take by force. In her dank bed she would tally her losses and wonder at his, trying to imagine what left holes so big that the only thing to staunch the bleeding was to steal whatever was around.

She heard his sister died. She thought to contact him but didn't. Years passed and technology changed. She spent drunken nights chasing him down rabbit holes—looking for him on social media, scouring papers, obituaries, the Department of Corrective Services. There was nothing, not a trace. She had expected some atrocity, a random act of senseless violence. Sometimes in the dark she tried holding him, her breath quickening as she sunk her fingers into phantom skin. She grabbed at what she could but he passed right through her, wide-eyed, loping back into the bush.

Acid

Annabel Stafford

He is a beautiful boy. White hair, large brown eyes, limbs just stretching out of their toddler stage. There's still a fold and dimple here and there; he doesn't yet have that almost malnourished look the older ones get. His mother has brought him in for reflux. I can't recall having seen him before and I usually remember the boys. I don't see very many children but it's a big clinic and mothers are panicky; they'll take the first available doctor, even if he is corpulent and balding. In any case, I would remember Jake even if it was a one-off walk-in. He's quiet. Intense.

The mother tells me his acid started maybe six months ago. Jake was burping a lot and holding the base of his throat. That's how she noticed.

'Have you seen anyone about it?'

Her voice rises to a guilty wail. 'He won't admit anything is wrong!'

I nod reassuringly. Six months. Silly woman.

Suddenly, she looks hopeful. 'I asked him if it feels like it's burning when he holds his throat. He admits that.'

Now she smiles. Jake is kneeling on the floor, going half-heartedly through the toys in the plastic tub under the bed. There's not much choice; none of the books have covers and the toys stopped working years ago—cast offs from the doctors' kids.

The mother wonders whether it is all the tomato sauce Jake eats. He has it on everything. No, she can't stop him. God forbid she do some actual parenting and discipline the child. Instead, she wonders if it might be something to do with dairy. Her sister-in-law, who is into fad diets and energy healing, is sure it's dairy. I mean, *she* doesn't believe in any of that, but she does wonder. And Google told her it's just a growth thing, or a disease called gastro offalgitis something-or-other. She looks nervous.

'I know. Dr Google. But I only look at sites like the Mayo Clinic. Things like that.'

Oh. She is intelligent. She knows *The Mayo Clinic*.

'Does it happen at the same time each day?'

'I think,' she turns to the boy. 'It's sort of different times, isn't it Jakey?'

Jake looks up from a ripped picture book of *The Faraway Tree*. Pre-PC version: all Dicks and Fannies and the girls doing the housework. He looks like a Blyton character himself. A scab on his left knee, those huge eyes, that mop of white hair.

'Different times.'

'And does it come every day?' I ask him.

'No. Just sometimes.'

He doesn't speak like a baby, despite the mother's efforts. He is older than she gives him credit for. I can tell by the eyes.

'Oh, yes. He can go for months without it happening and then it's back again… I don't know what's different about those weeks. I mean, he's not eating anything different.'

'Still the tomato sauce?'

'Oh yes, he never stops with that.'

'You really shouldn't let him have so much. There are low sugar versions—'

'I have the low sugar one. I wouldn't let him have the normal one.'

'Why bring him in now?' I let that sink in a little. While she's wondering whether I'm attacking her parenting I ask whether something happened recently, to make her think it's more serious. She brightens.

'Last week, after gymnastics… so it must have been Monday. He actually vomited… and kept holding his throat… I asked if it was burning and he admitted it was, but he wouldn't say any more than that.'

Jake is absorbed in *The Faraway Tree*, murmuring to himself about Silky and Moonface. Most children who come in throw it to one side; they want Lightning McQueen or PJ Masks or whatever the latest marketing brand the algorithms of mass predictability have spewed out. Someone has obviously read it to him; he fingers the page reverently.

I tell the mother that sometimes these things can be p-s-y-c-h-o-l-o-g-i-c-a-l.

'Really? Everything I've read makes it sound completely mechanical, I mean, that's not the right word, but you know what I mean.'

She is more intelligent than I gave her credit for. 'Yes, you're right'

She beams.

'I meant his unwillingness to tell you about it. Sometimes the child, if he is sensitive, wants to protect his parents from worry...'

She nods. 'Poor little guy.' She pushes out her bottom lip.

'So it might be an idea for me to talk to him. You could wait just outside in the corridor. I'll keep the door open, of course...'

She is affronted by the idea that Jake might rather talk to me and not to her, but she seems reluctant to be taken for a helicopter parent. There's not much chance of that given she's let the child suffer gastroesophageal reflux for six months without bothering to see a doctor. She looks over at him sifting through the toy box under the bed, looks anxiously back at me. I nod. She nods.

'Okay. Jakey? Mummy is going out to the corridor so you and the doctor can chat. I'll be just outside the door, okay?'

Most four-year-olds get difficult at this point and usually I just relent and let the mother stay. Sometimes, it has to be said, with a degree of relief. I am, the literature would say, opportunistic. But Jake doesn't squawk, he merely looks up at his mother and gives her a smile that looks for all the world like it is he that is reassuring her—rare child!—and then goes back to his book.

I ask him to come and sit on the chair so I can check his throat and ears. 'You can bring the book, if you like.'

There is no smile for me but still, he obeys. His legs dangle from the chair and his shorts have caught up on one side. I check his ears, sweet and grubby from childish fingers. My breath tickles him and he shivers a little as I ask him questions. I ask him about the burning sensation, but the mother is right, he is almost monosyllabic on the topic. I do manage to elicit that it happened after gymnastics and at 'bunkenhead'. I have garnered enough to justify my need for a one-on-one.

The consult chair is in the corner of the room, so it's not visible from the corridor. I ask Jake to say ahh, so I can check his throat and risk brushing his lips with my finger. He glares at me.

'Sorry, champ.' I press the wooden tab down on his tongue. That glare, as if he knows me. Knows what I'm thinking.

'Your throat looks perfect,' I say. 'A perfectly handsome pink throat.'

'I know that,' he says. He looks up from the book, squints at me, as if I'm a Lego project missing a part and he's trying to figure out which one.

'But what about those times after gymnastics? It burned then, did it?'

He nods.

'Why didn't you want to tell mummy?'

'Because it's meant to.'

'Burn?'

'Yes.'

It's 13 past, only two minutes left of the consult. And the mother will be getting antsy.

'It's not meant to burn, champ. It hurts, doesn't it?' I am on the other consult chair, my knees just an inch from his thigh.

He nods pertly, as if it's a stupid question.

'Your mummy says you don't tell her about it when your throat burns. Don't you want to stop it hurting?'

'No.'

'No?'

'No.'

'You like it when it hurts?'

He shakes his head. There is no shyness in the movement, rather a weary irritation. Then he does the most extraordinary thing: he points at the clock. Surely he can't read the time. Still, he raises his whole right arm to point at the clock behind my desk. It is exactly on quarter past.

'Yes, you're right. We're almost done. I just need you to tell me why you don't want mummy to help.' I am genuinely curious now. A mystery! We don't get them very often, not real ones anyway. It makes a nice change from all the hypochondriacs and alcoholics in denial.

He turns and looks at me, a strand of hair falling in his left eye. He doesn't blink or twitch; he is still looking for that missing piece of Lego.

'Why don't you want to make it go away, Jake?'

'God gave it to me.'

Ah. Poor child. 'The acid?'

He nods, eyes still on mine. He's frowning. How is it that a child's frown is so pretty? Jake can't wrinkle his brow so he squints, eyelashes thick around narrowed dark eyes. He flares his little nostrils and pouts. I lower my voice so the mother can't hear.

'Who on earth told you *God* gave you acid?

'God.'

I almost laugh. Sweet boy!

'God did?'

'Yes.'

'But how do you know it was God? Did He tell you? Or did someone tell you He said that… at Sunday school maybe?'

He shakes his head, from left to right, just once, slowly.

'Sometimes, when people tell us scary things, we can imagine them, so they seem very real. But they're not real.'

He turns a page of *The Faraway Tree.*

His lips turn down at the edges, fleshy at the centre. I touch his soft thigh; a reassuring hand against whatever misinformation he's being peddled and made to believe. His jaw shifts to one side, as if he is trying to get a piece of food from a back molar, but then further. Too far. A click, a movement, and his mouth, those beautiful lips, are stretching, stretching wider and wider. Too wide, so wide his jaw is dislocating. His eyes are closed, pushed back on the top of his head, slits now, to make way for the mouth.

My hand is still around his leg, my face a ruler length from that enormous mouth, but I can't move. And I see. At first particles down where the tonsils should be, like fine mist, but then they swarm and amass, pink like sputum, now red, red, clear, blue. Fire. Fire. My hand, oh Jesus Christ, my hands are on fire and my face? The smell. The smell of burnt flesh.

I run to the nurse's room, my hands burning. Tap on, tap on! Oh Jesus Christ the water burns, the skin, my skin, comes off in a layer, just lifts off. Pistons of pain shoot up through my palms up through the arms into my chest. Heat so hot it's like cold only Jesus Christ the pain…

I'm lying on the floor below the sink. The nurse tries to sit me up

'DON'T TOUCH MY HANDS.'

There is an infernal noise, the grating of an unoiled engine, round and round, dipping and rising and then I realise it's a scream and that it's coming from me. I can't stop it. It keeps playing, looping. In the door frame, through the bodies of the nurses and doctors, I see a flash of blonde. The boy's right arm is raised, someone is holding it, someone outside the frame. They're trying to pull him away, 'Don't stare darling'. He's not staring; only looking at me sadly. He has seen me: he knows what I am. With his free had he holds the base of his throat.

A Name like For Ever

Suzanne Hermanoczki

My name sounds like ever, like it will keep going on and on and never stop. Sometimes I feel like running out the front door of our hot ugly school, down the street, past our house and the row of wooden houses with those *barrio* dogs that hide in the shade by the front fence and chase you up and down one after another with their *loco*-dog-barking, running all the way down the hill, past the little corner shop at the end of Poinsettia Road, with its big windows and brightly candy-coloured plastic strips that dance to the breeze in the doorway, go round the corner, and past el creek full of cane toads. I'll run non-stop right outta *el suburbio* till I don't know where I am anymore, only stopping when I reach the end of the world!

When Ma orders me to do the washing up or hang out the clothes or set the table in Spanish, it's always *Eva*, as in *never*. When Pa says it in his funny sounding-mixed-up-Hungarian-Spanish, it's long and slow like the first letter got stuck somewhere in his mouth and is taking its time like for-*ever* to come out. But when my best mate Rosie Hickey from two streets away calls over the back fence, my name begins with a high 'e' the same as in me and gets longer and longer the more she has to wait at the fence for me to ride over to her house.

But ever since that first day at my new Catholic school (the posh one, Rosie says), all the *chicos* in my class copy that *estúpida* Mrs White, my teacher from grade three who got my name all wrong first.

'I simply don't understand you. Now, listen. *IInn-Eengliisshh-thiiss-iiss-hooww-wee-woould-saayy-yourr-naame.*'

She says this real slow, correcting all my sounds and even changing the last letter I've written on the page to an 'e'.

'Okay children, repeat after me, *Eeeeeeeeevvvvvve.*'

'*Eeeeeeeeevvvvvve.*'

'E-V-E,' Mrs White says. 'As in Christmas Eve,' she pats me on my head like a dog, then smiles. There's lipstick smudged all over her front teeth. 'Isn't she lucky, children?' she says to the rest of the class. 'Yes, she is. Sheee isss verrrrr-rrrryyyy lucccck-kyyyyyyy.'

I try to smile back, but my lips don't seem to work. Especially not now with all the other *chicos* in my class staring and laughing and saying my name over and over again all slow and *estúpido*-like. Instead, I look down at my new name which I don't think is lucky at all!

'Now everyone,' Mrs White says, turning around to speak to the class. 'I want you to be extra nice to Eve because she's not from here. I want you to help her because she doesn't know how to speak good English like the rest of us.'

'Miss, what's the matter with her? Why can't she speak?'

'Miss, Miss. She stupid or something?'

'Miss, is she a stupid wog?'

'Ha! Ha! Yeah, a stupid wog!'

'Stupid wog!'

'Stupid...'

'Shoosh! That's enough now children. Poor thing, I don't even think she understands a word we're saying. Maybe she needs to go to the special class.'

'Miss, will she need to catch the special bus then with all the special kids?'

'Ergh!'

'I'm not sitting next to her!'

'Me neither!'

The boys all snicker.

'That's enough! Eve, now come and sit by my desk. Here, right next to me.'

When she says that, it's all I can do to keep myself from crying like *un bebé*, or running right back outta that classroom, or worse, from throwing up all over the floor cos that's how sick it makes me feel.

Ever since then, I don't bother telling any of them where I'm from or what language I speak or what my real name is or *nada*, cos I know they'll never, *ever* EVER understand.

Every day since that terrible first day of school, I'm the first one outta that classroom when the bell rings at 3:00. At 3:06pm, I'm already on the school bus, sitting at my seat in the third row from the front, away from the big bad boys in the back row, waiting for the bus to start so it can take me all the way home.

Then, one day I'm sitting there, just looking out the window, when la Kylie England from *mi clase* speaks to me. Kylie, with her long, straight blonde plaits and bottle green ribbons tied in neat little bows and her forever shiny brown school shoes who lives on the good side of *el suburbio*, and always sits in the back row, asks to sit next to me! Kylie England, who lives in the big, new yellow-brick house with the super green grass and pretty pink-and-white *flores* hanging in baskets all the way round. It's la Kay-ah-lee Een-ga-land, whose *mamá* is always there every afternoon, waiting and waving for her when she gets off the bus. Señora England (that's her *mamá*), has the same blue eyes as la Kylie but her dark brown hair is cut short like la Princesa Diana's, complete with flicked-up waves. Every afternoon, Señora England stands by the white wooden fence in her sun visor hat and flowery garden gloves waiting for her. She is always smiling and bright like a summer's day not like my Ma, whose face reminds me of dark thunder clouds before they explode with rain.

'Can I sit here?' la Kylie asks again.

I close my gaping mouth and nod.

She smiles, showing me her perfectly straight white teeth.

I say nothing as la Kylie squashes in too close to the seat next to me.

'Here, wanna lollie?'

La Kylie pulls out a white paper bag from the side pocket of her school *uniforme* and shows me the warm soft milk bottle *caramelos* inside. She eats one, takes another out and puts it in my lap. The top of it is squished flat. La Kylie smiles again. I avoid her eyes and concentrate on the yellow freckles sprinkled across her nose and pretend they are a field of dandelions.

Then the bus starts its engine and lurches forward. All us *chicos* are thrown roughly back in our seats. Warm air blows on my face from a crack in the little rattling, sliding window square beside my head, as the bus slowly drives down the backstreets, moving away from school. I close my eyes and try to not to think about *el día* gone by, not understanding anything much in class, not playing with anyone at lunch, just pretending in my head. Not feeling the *aire* getting thicker and warmer inside the bus, or the boys' nasty remarks, their teasing getting louder, egging la Kylie to talk to me. I try to ignore her hot, heavy weight as she leans on my arm every time the bus turns the corners and swallowing deep, I try not to think of my old home, my old school, my old *amigos* from far, far away. I try to forget too that awful feeling growing deep in my belly.

With my eyes still closed, I concentrate on the sounds of the bus crunching its gears as it turns left onto the main road, listening to its growling engine as the bus picks up speed. Soon, we are flying down the hill on our way home. Inside the bus, the noise starts getting louder with *chicos* from all classes shouting and yelling at each other from across the seats. Some of my little brother Attie's friends in the front rows, have taken out their recorders and have started playing *Waltzing Matilda*. From the back of the bus, comes the sound of paper being ripped out of exercise books. Those sounds come from the older, rough boys like Scotty Mudge and Mickey Lancaster who smell of sweat and pee and dirt, and are always swearing and getting into fights and teasing and calling people names. Even with my eyes shut, I can picture them in their untucked shirts, their grubby hands reaching into their stinking school bags as they start preparing for their afternoon spit ball wars. My eyes are closed tight when a tiny voice whispers in my ear.

'Hey, what's your name?'

I open my eyes and turn around, but no one is talking. Beside me, la Kylie looks straight ahead. I lean my head on the glass and stare out the window. I shut my eyes again. I must have imagined it.

'Psst!'

The voice whispers again, but this time I keep my eyes closed.

'Hey, I said, tell me your name – the way you said it that first day in class...'

I turn around. That's when I notice la Kylie's lips are moving. She's looking straight ahead but it's her voice. She's speaking ever so softly. I can't understand her too well.

I'm about to turn away again when she squeezes my arm.

'C'mon! I just wanna hear how you said it to Mrs White on that first day of school, that's all.'

When she grips my arm tighter, I start shaking my head. Her fingernails dig a little too hard into my flesh, but when she turns to face me, she smiles. I sit there hypnotized by her bluest of blue eyes. My lips part, but I don't say anything. That's when la Kylie leans in, her head is so close, it's almost touching mine.

'You can whisper it to me, like a secret. It's okay, just *say-your-name*,' she says, slowly, sweetly, her voice like a song.

I shake my head and hold my belly and look out the window again. I take big breaths and concentrate on the broken lines of fences going past – *uno, dos, tres* – but she keeps interrupting, asking for my name.

'Oh, c'mon!' la Kylie says. 'I'm being nice to you, sitting next to you and everything! I even gave you a lollie!' She pinches my arm. I try to ignore her sharp little fingernails scratching my skin and the churning feeling growing deep inside *mi estomago*.

I close my eyes and swallow again, trying to block out the bus with its noises and bad smells and sounds. I try to ignore la Kylie as she pleads, begs for me to speak. How I hate her bony fingers that keep touching my skin and the sound of her voice in my ear, hot and sticky. I am ready to push her away and tell her to leave me alone for good, I'm not feeling well, when something warm brushes against my cheek. I turn my head from the window and look down, surprised to see her resting her golden head on my shoulder.

'Oh, c'mon pretty please, can't you just say your name?' she murmurs. 'It can be our secret. Yours and mine.'

And before I know it, my lips pull apart slowly. Maybe, I think, if I tell her, then she'll understand and she'll ask me to sit with her at big lunch and I'll be her friend, *su amiga!*

'*En español me llamo Eva,*' I whisper quickly in Spanish.

'What?' la Kylie slowly lifts her head and stares at me. I know she's holding her breath so she can hear me speak better.

I pull back.

'I didn't mean to … I mean, please, say it again,' la Kylie says with a smile.

I swallow. '*En español* … you ah say Eva,' I repeat in my broken-up English. 'But *en inglés* you can say to me, *Evita.*' As I speak the last bit, I return her smile.

La Kylie stares at me wide-eyed before breaking into a dazzling smile. I feel my heart jump and my lips curling up higher and higher. Then, without warning, she stands up and turns around quick-fast.

'Hey boooooooooooooyyyyysssssssssssssssssssss!'

I follow to where she's looking at and feel my stomach drop to the ground and roll over. I catch her waving at the bad boys in my class and the big bullies from the older years—and in a flash all the rough boys in the back rows stop throwing spit balls at each other.

Several pairs of love-struck eyes all follow la Kylie as she stands up.

Knowing the boys are watching her, she walks down the aisle with her school bag. In the middle of the bus, she stops and puts down her bag. With a flick of golden hair over her shoulder, she straightens up and flashes the boys a smile so wide, they look close to fainting.

'Bye-bye *Eeee-vah*,' Kylie waves and glances over her shoulder in my direction.

Everyone on the bus turns to gawk at me.

I gulp hard and sink down lower in my seat.

'I said, 'Bye-bye E-viiiii-*taaaaahhh*.'

I pretend not to hear her say my name like that and instead look down at my feet. I bite on my bottom lip to stop it shaking, but she's already seen it wobble.

'*Awwwww*. Are you crying, Evita?' la Kylie pretends to sniff into a hankie. 'Aw. Don't cry for me.'

A couple of *chicos* start to snicker.

'Aw. What's-a matter, Evittaaaahhhhhh?' she says, louder and meaner now.

More *chicos* turn around. Some even laugh. Those in the front row (my brother Attie included) have stopped playing their recorders and have turned round to listen.

'Hey Evita, I said, What's the matter with you? Hey?'

All the bad boys break out into fits of laughter while Kylie grins. Before long, they are sitting up straight and staring at la Kylie who is waving her hands in the air like *una directora de orquesta*.

How she smiles at those loud-mouthed love-struck boys when they start belting out the words to *that* song, the one *she* wanted me and everyone on the bus to hear.

Then, Kylie pauses a beat with both hands lifted in the air. The boys in the back row wait, and on her signal, all jump up, belting out the last line of the song and pointing their fingers at me.

'Ah-why don't you get outta this place!'

When they finish, they fall about laughing. La Kylie turns and flashes me her whitest smile, the same one I wish I could smash into tiny little pieces.

But then, out of nowhere, the bus slams on its brakes.

I feel myself sliding down into my seat, while all around me *chicos* are bumping their heads against the metal hand rails and windows.

A couple of *chicos* from the back row yelp as they are sent flying down the aisle. But la Kylie holds on tight, and slips into a spare seat, just in time.

'Quiiiiiiiiiiieeeeeeeeeeeeeeeeeeeeeeeeeeeeeeeeeeeeeeeeeeeeeeeettt ttttttttt!'

Mr Mudge the bus-driver yells so loud and long that by the time I pull myself up again, his face has changed from bright red to purple. He stops. He glares at each one of us as he catches his breath. His breathing is loud and heavy, and his fat face is dripping with sweat. His blue-checked shirt that's stretched tight across his huge belly, is stuck to the back of his meaty neck. He reminds me of *un toro* in a bullfighting ring staring at *el matador*—big, angry, tired and real crazy-mad.

'NOW-SIT-DOWN-AND-Shut-yer-traps-or-every-last-one-of-youse-will-be- walking-home! ya-hear-me?'

No one speaks.

No one moves.

A couple of grade-oners in the first-row start crying but after a bit of shooshing, nobody, not even Attie says anything, but I can tell he's close to crying too. I bite down on my trembling lips and stare at Mr Mudge's angry face; for *un segundo*, he looks straight at me but all I can see is the blue vein in the middle of his forehead which has popped out.

En silencio, the whole bus watches him take out a handkerchief and mop the sweat from his brow.

'Now,' he asks gruffly, opening the door. 'Which one of youse is getting off?'

Quickly, quietly, la Kylie rises out of her seat while everyone watches. Picking up her school bag, she walks to the front of the bus, carefully stepping over bags and books and *chicos* strewn all over the floor. When she reaches Mr Mudge, she pauses.

'Thank you, Mr Mudge,' she says, softly. 'And God Bless you.'

Mr Mudge grunts.

A hundred eyes all follow la Kylie as she gets off the bus.

Then, the whispers start.

'Ergh. She sat next to that stinking wog!' Scotty Mudge remarks.

'Her mum better hose her off quick!' his friend Mickey Lancaster adds.

'Yeah! Wash that wog stink off!' Scotty Mudge says in disgust.

That terrible feeling creeps back, this time reaching deep inside to grip *mi corazón*.

As I watch la Kylie exit the bus, tears well up in my eyes. I try to hold them back but this time, they don't stop. I try to breathe, but I can't. I place a hand on the little glass square near my head and start pushing and pushing against the window wishing for it to slide open so I can get some fresh air, some *buenos aires*, when I see a hand, a flowery white glove lift high up into the sky in front of my eyes.

Outside, the whole world slows down like in slow-motion.

My eyes move from la Kylie then back to la Señora England's gloved hand which is floating like a puffy little cloud, gliding backwards and forwards, backwards and forwards.

As the bus pulls away from the curb, and the noise on the bus slowly starts up again, la Señora England's bluest of blue of eyes catch onto mine.

As she stands there next to la Kylie, she beams so radiantly while she waggles her gloved hand at me.

And for *un segundo* before I throw up, for a split *momentito*, la Señora England looks exactly like the Queen.

The Sea Wife

Sophie Overett

She wore white to their wedding like every other bride he knows, but no other bride was half drowned in sea water, salt collecting behind her ears like perfume, seaweed settling in a noose around her neck. Her legs beat at the water and she'd laughed at him, of course she had, her head back, her pale neck long, disappearing down beneath the transparent lace of her dress. He had wanted to lay his head there, hold her close, feel her breath, her heart, the stutter echoing in her chest as she spoke. As it was though, he had just kicked off his shoes, felt them sink heavily to the sea floor, felt the loss of them at his toes and at the soles of his wide feet. Her hand had reached for his tie, then the lapel of his jacket, as she drowned him with her.

From the kitchen of the lighthouse he can see her. The filmy cotton of her night dress hanging loose over her thin body, her long legs like anchors slung below. More from memory than sight, he sees the veins that run deep beneath her skin, unrelenting as a network of rivers.

They have edged out of Tasmania's dry summer in the last few weeks, the change of season coaxing in the sea winds and the blanketing fog. The last few days have been marked by both, and Miri had ignored it until this morning.

'I'll tell it to quieten down,' she'd whispered into the galley of his neck, rousing him from his slumber. He'd gone back to sleep, woken hours later to find Miri out there, spitting words off the cliff while the wind got its hooks in her, tearing at her dress, her hair, at the long, stark line of her.

Frank stands by the kitchen sink, watching her with the sort of audience one gives a film they've seen too many times before. He takes another sip of his coffee, tastes the bitter grounds at his tongue, at the roof of his mouth.

They are not young anymore. Time has beaten her as it has him, stooped their backs and dug trenches in their skin, left them craggy jawed and sallow eyed. He flexes his hand around the mug, feels the arthritis stiffen in his fingers. The magpies are calling now, long-beaked glimmers of black and white through the fog. He sees one land hard on the grass, shake out its stick legs and step forwards beneath the haze of mist. It stops. Sharpens its beak on a stone. He's distracted enough he almost misses Miri stagger. The wind, just for an instance, beckoning her instead of pushing.

Frank jerks forwards, like there's a chance he could reach her before her knees hit the ground, but she regains her footing. She spins quickly on the spot though, and turns to face him, smiling, like she'd heard his palpating heart all those metres away.

His hands tremble, and he thinks this is enough, that it's time, and pours her a mug of black coffee. Leaves the lighthouse kitchen to meet her.

'We should go to the beach today,' she says, her voice heavy as a tarp after a downpour. Frank doesn't need to speak to agree.

They'd married back in the spring of '63 on the deck of her father's boat. It had been a modest crowd. His mother was dead, his father a drunk, and he'd had only his former employer in the crowd, a barrel-chested man with the wide set eyes of a lizard.

Frank had worn the uniform he'd soon leave in, scrubbed green and stiff, still starchy from the box it had arrived in. If Miri had noticed, she hadn't commented, her fingers wrapped tight around a bouquet of bougainvillea, the auburn hair at the back of her neck frizzy from where the humidity and seawater pulled at it. She had been such a mystery then, the lighthouse keeper's daughter, with her bee-stung lips and the knowing look in her eye, the gaze of a woman far beyond her years.

The beach is barely a beach, rather a small line of sand which reaches out and holds the water at bay like a cupped hand. It is down past the lighthouse and it takes them an hour to walk the distance, age telling in their shuffling.

They arrive in the heat of the morning, the salt off the sea like seasoning on their tongues. He licks it off his teeth. He's never liked it much but Miri swallows it whole. The taste of it filling her up until she basks, lazy and sated, on the sand, warming beneath the afternoon sun. The winds are quieter down here, off the cliff face, the fog lost above them and further out across the sea.

They met at a military fundraiser aboard her father's ship where Frank was working as a deckhand. Miri's father, Mr. Glass, had always been a stern man, but the grief from the death of his wife and the burden of having served in two wars had left him so full that he seemed to overflow suddenly and sharply at inopportune moments, breaking down with a hand to his head, letting the tears drop thick, catching in the collar of his uniform. Miri seemed to alternate then between tending to the damage and running away from it, and on this night Mr. Glass had gotten drunk on gin and vermouth while Miri had left him to it, instead hanging herself over the edge of the docked ship and letting the water lap at her bare legs. She had ignored her father and the party but not the sea and Frank Wiley had fallen horribly, heartbreakingly in love.

Across the sand now, Miri looks at him like she did then, curious and bright, like she wants to pry open his closed look and dip inside. He shifts away from her and glances out at the water instead, at the way it seems to follow her, curl around the corner of beach where she's set up for the morning. It speaks to her, and Frank sees her shift her gaze from him to the water, like she's heard it, like she's listening, and wants it to know she is. Like she's married to it and not him. In some ways, he guesses she is.

You courted people back then. He'd been so young and he'd followed her every move, certain in his infatuation. It was not until the spring that he would kiss her, that she would give any hint of reciprocating his affection. They had been at sea for a day, Frank having worked his way into her father's esteem, and before they had even docked she had leapt from the side of the ship. Blindly, he had followed, launching his body over the side, desperate to reach her before they broke the line of the ocean. He doesn't remember what happened, doesn't recall the crash, or the crush of the water, but he remembers opening his eyes to the burn of the sea and meeting Miri. Her own eyes had been wide and wild and on him and her mouth thinned like a fishing line, until both her eyes and her mouth cut into smiling crescents. She had kissed him then beneath beating waves and he had breathed again from her, like sucking on the mouth of an oxygen tank. He was a young man, and holding him, she had been as timeless as the water they kneaded beneath themselves to stay put.

He reads about it sometimes. Women from the ocean. Sirens and mermaids and selkies, all with vicious pulls in them to coax men from the safety of land and into foreign depths. A rip with lush hair and full, soft breasts. But that's not Miri. She never coaxed him anywhere, but rather he's kept her here, holding onto her like a child with a net, catching insects or urchins, pulsing, writhing, living and wild.

On the beach, the sun is brutal and Frank shields his eyes from the glare as he glances back up at the tumbling cliff. He can see the lighthouse from here, a tall, narrow thing with white walls and a hollow centre that rips up the middle like the barrel of a gun. Frank knows this, because he has handled many.

He had not been familiar with lighthouses when his father-in-law had taken his ship out to sea, never to return, but the war had that effect, of locking people out of old lives and handing them the keys to new ones. Even with the sun, the glow from the lighthouse is startling from down here, the beacon it's meant to be, that he forgets it is, and he glances at Miri to see if she's noticed it too. When he shifts his gaze though, she's looking at him, an affectionate twist to her expression that still makes his heart stutter. She's in the water now, waist deep and her hands light on the surface of it, trembling slightly, and he wants to go over, reach out and cover them with his own hands, but knows she wouldn't want it.

Her fingers are cold on his scars.

'Shot here,' he'd told her, where the graze has dug a grave in his skin. Her fingers dip into it, cold to the touch, and he watches her face and feels her trail up to his shoulder and down his chest, the jail bars of his ribs, then back up. There are starbursts of freckles there, exploding behind the full moons of his nipples. The fine hair on his arms, chest, back, rubbed raw from the stress of his uniform and the heavy packs that had weighed him down for his first rotation and then his second.

Miri doesn't reply. Her eyebrows are furrowed, her face lined with worry, so he forgets the war and tells her about the water in Vietnam. The brown, rainwater they gulped out of puddles and the muddy Rung Tal swamps and then, finally, the impossible blue of Vung Tau. Electric or royal, close to navy some nights, not like Tasmania's Indian Ocean, all vibrant, teals or pretty moss greens.

'Are you that one as well?' he'd asked. 'Was it you I waded through? Drank from?'

He talks until his throat is raw and Miri leans forwards to kiss the words out of his mouth, to lick them from the backs of his teeth, and her mouth is as cold as the sea had been, all those years ago.

There are nightmares of course. Frank is not a natural killer, but he'd shot the lanky, too-young boys as fast as they'd come, through their eyes or necks, once in the knee. He had felt such a man before he'd left, but here he was a boy playing at manhood, his hands wrapped around a bayonet he barely knew how to use.

He dreams of the boys he killed, the men. Imagines their widows and wonders if they imagine the dead Australian men too. 'There are no villains here,' another boy had said. 'Just cannon fodder.'

He doesn't tell Miri about the dreams, but she's there when he wakes up anyway, the moon gleaming through the window and the terror locking his chest and throat shut.

She holds him, in her arms and on land, crawling into their bed and kissing him all over with wet, cold lips. Shaking, he would reach out for her and she would not stray, would sing him to her like a siren. He would rest against her and she would be the one to anchor them to this life for a change.

She was not always beside him when he woke.

Too many times, he had shaken awake from nightmares alone, throat hoarse from yelling, his cries unanswered, his hands reaching for twisted, vacant sheets beside him. Sometimes she was watching from the window, from the door, other times gone from their room altogether. One bleak night, he had startled upright to the slam of the lighthouse door, and then to her running, running, running out across the cliff.

He'd sprung from his bed, made chase, only to see her leap from the edge, disappear from the surface in a billow of a white nightgown and a shock of auburn hair.

Panic had seized him, but not paralysed him, and he had sprung down the steps to the beach and sailed his dingy out, braving the reckless sea for her. He had cast out his old fishing net, and finally, impossible hours later, he had snared her.

She had struggled violently against him before lying flat on the floor of the boat, gasping like the salmon he caught with his father as a boy. He had found himself leaning back and away from her, almost over the side of the boat, until she stopped dead, her skin pale and her body limp. Fumbling, he had touched her icy skin, gripped her arms, pulled her prostrate body to the edge of the boat and watched her gasp back to life as the waves slammed against the side of the boat like icy hands.

At home he had undressed her, ready to tend to wounds that weren't there, and finally he had left her in bed, wrapped in damp towels with seaweed at her ankles and through her hair, stinking of salt and sand and water. He slept restlessly on the couch downstairs until she found him, sought him out. Her lips were blue as she said, 'I will always pick you.'

He kicks off his sandals and slides down his trousers until he is as naked as he knows she is, kicking her old legs loosely in the sea. He wades out after her, and catches her startled look, keeps it locked up in his head. Frank is not a strong swimmer, never was, and he rarely comes out here with her, much more inclined to rest on the shore.

The water's close to frigid, but the closer he gets to her, the warmer it is. He wonders if it's her doing, if this is the invitation so often there, in the twist of her lips or the soft rivers of veins below her skin.

When he reaches her, he kisses her at the corner of her mouth and then on her thin lips. She stops, treads water until she's not, until she's curling her legs between his and they're both still there, not sinking like they should be.

Overhead, a helicopter chops, beats it's propellers, slicing the air above them and he's here until he's not, until the memory of the war, the blood of his friends on his clothes and beneath his nails is in him, churning beneath the current like sand off the sea floor. The breath is caught in his throat, hooked on a line. It is long seconds before he is back, Miri's soft hand on his elbow, the other around his neck.

'Where'd you go, mister?' she sings, and this time, when he kisses her he hears it. The roar of the sea there, like pressing the lips of a sea shell to his weathered ear.

Biographies

Julia Prendergast is a Senior Lecturer in Writing and Literature (Swinburne University, Melbourne). She is the current Chair of the Australasian Association of Writing Programs (AAWP), the peak academic body representing the discipline of Creative Writing in Australasia. Julia's novel, *The Earth Does Not Get Fat* was published in 2018 (UWA Publishing: Australia). Her short stories feature in the current edition of *Australian Short Stories* (Pascoe Publishing). Other stories have been recognised and published: *Lightship Anthology 2* (UK), *Glimmer Train* (US), *TEXT* (AU), Séan Ó Faoláin Competition (IE), Review of Australian Fiction. Julia's research appears in *New Writing* (UK) and *TEXT* (AU).

Joshua Kemp is an author of Australian gothic fiction. His short stories have been published by literary journals such as *Overland*, *Kill Your Darlings*, *Seizure*, *Tincture* and *Breach*. His story 'Pigdog' appeared in the first *ACE Anthology*. Last year he was longlisted for the Fogarty Literary Award and this year he was shortlisted for the Kill Your Darlings Unpublished Manuscript Award.

Margaret Hickey is an award-winning playwright and author. She holds a PhD in Australian literature and is a lecturer at La Trobe University. Marg is a regular guest on ABC radio and is a judge for the Joseph Furphy literature prize. She lives in North East Victoria with her husband and three sons. 'Glory Days' appears in Marg's short story collection *Rural Dreams* (MidnightSun Publishing: 2020). Marg was the 2018 winner of the Australasian Association of Writing Programs (AAWP) / Australian Short Story Festival (ASSF) Emerging Writers' Short Story Award.

Joshua Hayes is from the Barossa Valley in South Australia. This year has seen him treed by the Pandemic and living in his mother's basement. He enjoys birdwatching and is considering taking up taxidermy. You can find his trunk writing at fleshpunk.com, a website he had the wherewithal to create, but not the enthusiasm to maintain.

Deb Wain is a poet and short story writer who lives and writes on Taungurung Country in Central Victoria and who is passionate about food, culture, and the Australian environment. She has generally been employed in jobs where she is allowed to talk and tell stories for a living. When not writing or talking, you can find Deb playing with her dogs, drinking coffee, or poking about in the garden. Her work, which has appeared in *Meniscus*, *Colloquy*, *Verandah*, *Tincture*, and *Verity La*, is often inspired by the Australian communities in which she has lived.

Anne Hotta is an Australian, resident in Melbourne. She is a teacher and an aspiring author of the short story. Some stories have been published and awarded. 'Kanreki' (featured in this collection) was the 2019 winner of the Australasian Association of Writing Programs (AAWP) / Australian Short Story Festival (ASSF) Emerging Writers' Short Story Award. *Overland* has published three stories. *Kill Your Darlings* included a story in their 2019 anthology, *New Australian Fiction*. Other awards include the Lorian Hemmingway Short Story Competition (second place, 2018) and the Rockingham Open Short Story Award (first place 2015) Anne is the recipient of two Varuna Writing Centre Fellowships.

Judi Morison is of Gamilaroi and Celtic heritage and writes fiction, creative nonfiction and poetry. She is working on a second novel while waiting for a publisher to snap up her first. Judi is editorial assistant for *Dreaming Inside: Voices from Junee Correctional Centre*, an annual anthology of writing by Aboriginal inmates.

Thomas Hamlyn-Harris is a book designer, illustrator and writer of comics and short fiction. His work has been published in comic anthologies, games, animations, magazines, children's fiction, pop-up books and nonfiction puzzle and activity books. He lectures and tutors in design and illustration at the University of the Sunshine Coast.

Chemutai Glasheen lives in Western Australia. She is a teacher and a sessional academic at Curtin University. She writes fiction for young people and her work is influenced by her interest and experience in human rights and education. She has written a collection of short stories which are set in east Africa (unpublished). She holds a PhD from Curtin University in creative writing. Her research explores the role of fiction in raising awareness about human rights.

Carly Rawson is an emerging writer studying in the Creative Writing program at Swinburne University. She has recently abandoned the city for the coast, carried upon the tide of inevitable returns to her birthplace. She enjoys water, wind and clean empty spaces. She has been published in *Other Terrain, Chart Collective* and the *Big Issue*.

Annabel Stafford has a Doctor of Creative Arts from UTS, where she teaches in the Creative Writing program. Annabel previously worked as Sydney Correspondent for *The Age* newspaper and as a Canberra political reporter for *The Age* and *The Australian Financial Review*. Her writing has been published in *The Best Australian Science Writing 2019, The Good Weekend, The Griffith Review, The*

Sydney Morning Herald, Meanjin, The Tablet, Inside Story and *La Hoja de Arena.*

Suzanne Hermanoczki is a writer and teacher of creative writing. Her writing on death and photography, trauma and the immigrant journey, memory and postmemories, code-switching and bi/multi-cultural identity, Latinx, gringos and magic realism, have been published in local and international publications including, *Australian Multilingual Writing Project, Cha: An Asian Literary Journal, TEXT* and *Verge Anthology.* Highly commended in 2018 for the *AAWP/ASSF Short Story Prize* and winner of the 2014 inaugural *Affirm Press Creative Writing Prize,* she has written two novels (seeking publication). She holds a PhD and Masters in Creative Writing from the University of Melbourne, where she works.

Sophie Overett is an award-winning writer and cultural producer. Her stories have been published in *Griffith Review, Going Down Swinging, Overland* Online, *The Sleepers Almanac,* and elsewhere. She won the 2020 Penguin Literary Prize, the 2018 AAWP x UWRF Emerging Writers' Prize, and her work has been shortlisted for multiple other awards including The Text Prize and The Richell Prize. She is one half of Lady Parts, a podcast about women's roles in genre cinema, and her novel, *The Rabbits,* will soon be published by Penguin Random House Australia. You can find her at https://protect-au.mimecast.com/s/W-uwCxnMOnFqnpoA-S8utnl?domain=sophieoverett.com.

Acknowledgements

I would like to thank Shane Strange at Recent Work Press, for publishing this collection and for being 'the real deal'. I include an extract from the Recent Work Press website as case in point:

> Our authors are our partners. We are careful about selecting the writers we work with. Often they are asked personally to submit work, or to participate in an anthology. We believe in them as writers and artists and we want to share our collaborative success.

I would also like to acknowledge the generous support of the Australasian Association of Writing Programs, for financially supporting this anthology.

Warm thanks to the Australasian Association of Writing Programs, together with our partner organisations: the Australian Short Story Festival, Ubud Writers and Readers Festival, and the University of Western Australia Publishing, for unwavering commitment to providing prizes and publication pathways for emerging writers. The authors featured in this collection were identified through these initiatives.

Thank you to the Australasian Association of Writing Programs, Partnerships and Prizes team: Katrina Finalyson, Dominique Hecq, Luke Johnson, Daniel Juckes and Jen Webb.

Finally, and crucially, thank you to the authors in this collection—it has been my privilege and my pleasure to work with each of you, and your ACE stories.